P9-DVO-309

# IT TAKES TWO

# Go! Fight! Twin!

by Belle Payton

Simon Spotlight

New York   London   Toronto   Sydney   New Delhi

This book is a work of fiction. Any references to historical events, real people, or real places are used fictitiously. Other names, characters, places, and events are the product of the author's imagination, and any resemblance to actual events or places or persons, living or dead, is entirely coincidental.

SIMON SPOTLIGHT
An imprint of Simon & Schuster Children's Publishing Division
1230 Avenue of the Americas, New York, New York 10020
This Simon Spotlight edition October 2014
© 2014 by Simon & Schuster, Inc. All rights reserved, including the right of reproduction in whole or in part in any form.
SIMON SPOTLIGHT and colophon are registered trademarks of Simon & Schuster, Inc.
Text by Sarah Albee
Designed by Ciara Gay
For information about special discounts for bulk purchases, please contact Simon & Schuster Special Sales at 1-866-506-1949 or business@simonandschuster.com.
Manufactured in the United States of America 0914 FFG
10 9 8 7 6 5 4 3 2 1
ISBN 978-1-4814-1655-9 (pbk)
ISBN 978-1-4814-1656-6 (hc)
ISBN 978-1-4814-1657-3 (eBook)
Library of Congress Catalog Card Number 2013955432

# CHAPTER ONE

*Bam! Bam! Bam! Bam!*

The bass drum player was pounding rhythmically to excite the crowd. The cheerleaders shouted and clapped and performed hair-raising acrobatics. Ava Sackett watched, holding her breath, as her friend Kylie McClaire's older sister, Yvette, stood on another girl's shoulders high above the ground and then pointed one leg up into the air.

But then the opposing team scored another field goal, and the Ashland Tigers' fans lapsed into a despondent silence. The Tigers were losing by seventeen points, and there were only seven minutes left in the game.

From her seat high in the stands, Ava looked

down at her older brother, Tommy. He stood on the sidelines with the rest of his teammates, dejectedly watching what was happening on the field. His helmet was off, and when he turned his head, she could see his thick brown hair drooping down over his eyes. Ava knew what he was thinking—not only was the team going to lose, but also there was no way he'd be going into the game.

Farther along the sideline was their father, Mike Sackett, who was the coach of the Ashland Tigers. His job was the reason their family had moved to Ashland, Texas, from the East Coast this summer. Ava watched as Coach stalked up and down the sideline in his Tigers jacket, communicating with his assistant coaches through the big headphones he wore. The assistant coaches were stationed in the tower high above the field, where they could watch the game.

The crowd groaned.

"What happened?" demanded Ava's friend Kylie. Kylie hadn't really paid attention to football before she and Ava became friends—she was more interested in things like jewelry making and fantasy novels—but Ava was teaching her how the game worked. To Ava's delight, Kylie seemed to enjoy football almost as much as Ava did.

"PJ misjudged the throw," said Ava. "Did you see how Tyler Whitley stopped and cut over toward the sideline? PJ's lucky it didn't get intercepted. It doesn't look good."

"Is there any way we can pull out a win?" asked Kylie.

"Highly doubtful." Ava watched Kylie's sister leap off two people's shoulders, land in a pike on their waiting arms, bounce up onto her feet, do a backbend, and finally land in a split. "Wow. Your sister is awesome."

"Wow. Kylie McClaire's sister is awesome," said Alex Sackett, who was sitting between Lindsey Davis and Emily Campbell, a few feet farther along the bleacher from her twin sister.

"She's amazing," agreed Emily.

Alex watched in fascination as Yvette stood on the shoulders of two teammates standing side by side, her arms up in a V. Then she pulled her right leg up from the side so it was touching her ear—all while standing on one foot on someone's shoulder.

"She's so flexible," said Alex.

"Well, at our level we don't do stuff like that," said Lindsey. "But we do a lot of choreographed routines. It just takes practice."

"I'm sure you could do it if you worked at it, Alex," said Emily. "You should try out for cheerleading with us."

"Yeah," agreed Lindsey. "You're from such an athletic family."

"Ha," said Alex. "Ava and Tommy inherited all the athletic genes." Not only was Tommy on the high school football team, but Ava had just made the middle school football team a few weeks ago. Alex noticed that Rosa Navarro, sitting on the other side of Lindsey, was listening intently to the conversation but not adding to it. Alex had heard Rosa was one of the best seventh grade cheerleaders. *Does she not think I have what it takes?* Alex wondered.

"It's a combination of dance, gymnastics, and tumbling," Emily said. "But not all of us do the big acrobatic tumbling stuff. That you really do need to have practiced from a young age."

"Rosa's our best tumbler," said Lindsey.

"Don't you think Alex should try out, Rosa?" asked Emily.

Rosa hesitated. "Well, not everyone is cut out for cheerleading," she said. "It takes a lot of coordination and flexibility."

Alex's eyes narrowed. What was that supposed to mean? Did Rosa think she was uncoordinated?

The roar of the opposing team's fans interrupted the conversation. The clock ran down. The Tigers had lost.

Alex was still busy thinking as everyone stood up to leave and her sister poked her arm.

"That was pretty grim," said Ava.

"Huh? What was grim?" asked Alex, puzzled.

Ava stared at her. "Uh, the game? The fact that we just lost?"

"Oh!" said Alex with a little laugh. "Right. Yeah, too bad. So are you going to Sal's?" The middle school kids usually gathered at the local pizza place after home games.

Ava frowned at her. "Yeah, I promised Kylie I'd head over with her," she said. "But I'm only staying for a little while—I want to rest up for my game tomorrow. I'll see you there?"

"Yep, sure," said Alex. She was still thinking about Rosa's remarks. Not that she had time to participate in sports, now that she was class president. And it was true that Alex herself commented all the time that she was uncoordinated athletically. But it was one thing for Alex to say it. It was quite another thing for someone else to agree with her, out loud, in front of everyone.

And honestly, cheerleading? How hard could it be?

# CHAPTER TWO

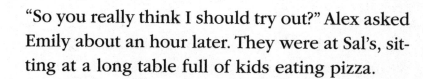

"So you really think I should try out?" Alex asked Emily about an hour later. They were at Sal's, sitting at a long table full of kids eating pizza.

"You totally should!" said Emily. They watched Sal, the owner, waltz around the room, refilling water glasses as he sang opera arias at the top of his lungs.

"Sports are not really my thing," said Alex. She glanced down the table. Toward the other end, Lindsey and Corey O'Sullivan sat side by side, talking in low voices to each other. They had been very close until a family fight pulled them apart, but recently they'd started being friendly toward each other again. Alex wasn't quite sure how she felt about it, but she was pretty sure she was glad—even if her heart did still speed up a little bit whenever she saw Corey.

"So, Alex, how psyched was Charlie when you told him you'd won the election?" asked their friend Annelise Mueller, who was sitting across from Alex.

"Charlie?" asked Alex blankly. Then she remembered. Charlie! Her phantom boyfriend! The one she'd told everyone she was going out with back home. Ugh! Alex knew she was a terrible liar. She was constantly forgetting what she'd told people and acting clueless when they repeated stuff she'd said to them. She had blurted out that she had a boyfriend named Charlie in a moment of panic, and now she regretted the lie every day. To further complicate things, *Ava* really did have a sort-of boyfriend back home named Charlie, although who knew what the status of that situation was. Alex needed to figure out how to spread the word that she had broken up with Charlie, and soon.

"Oh! Charlie!" she said with a laugh. "Yeah, um, he was really happy about it." She searched her brain for a way to quickly change the subject. "So, when are cheerleading tryouts again?"

"This Sunday," said Annelise. "Are you going to try out?"

"It does sound really fun, but I don't think so," said Alex. "Even if I wanted to be on the team, I wouldn't have time. Being class president is a big responsibility."

Rosa stopped chatting with Xander Browning, who was sitting across the table from her. "How are you planning to fulfill the sports requirement, then?" she asked.

Alex froze, a slice of pizza midway to her mouth. She set it back down. "What sports requirement?"

"Oh, didn't you know?" asked Emily. "Everyone has to participate in some sort of athletic activity for at least two seasons. It's part of the district's 'physical fitness initiative,'" she said, making air quotes with her fingers.

"That's totally ridiculous," said Alex. "My responsibilities as class president should exempt me from such a dumb rule."

Rosa snorted. "Being in student government does not begin to approach the time commitment that a real sport requires," she said.

The table had suddenly quieted down. Everyone seemed to be tuning in to Alex and Rosa's conversation.

Alex was aware that people were interested in what she would say about this. She looked for Ava. Ava was usually the one she relied on for navigating these tricky social situations. But Ava was sitting across the restaurant at a booth with Kylie and their friend Jack Valdeavano. They were laughing their heads off about something. Fleetingly, she wondered if Ava and Jack were becoming more than friends, but then she snapped back to the conversation at hand.

"Well," she said with a shrug, "believe that if you want, but I definitely don't have time to both be class president and do a sport. What if I volunteered to be the manager or something?"

Lindsey shook her head. "Even if you just want to be manager, you still have to try out for the team," she said. "At least for cheerleading. Coach Jen only takes managers who show an interest in the sport."

"Oh," said Alex dejectedly.

"You should totally just try out, Alex!" said Emily excitedly. "You have the perfect personality for it, and you get good grades, and you must be a natural athlete! Seriously, just look at your family."

Alex was intrigued. Lindsey and Emily genuinely seemed to want her to join the squad. And they were right, being athletic was in her genes. Really, she'd always been able to do just about anything she set her mind to. Why should cheerleading be any different? "Hmm," she mused. "I could—"

"She won't make it past the first cuts," snapped Rosa.

Alex's temper flared. "What if I do make the cut?" she demanded.

"Well, then you'll be all set," said Rosa with what Alex suspected was a tiny twinge of sarcasm. "Maybe Coach Jen will let you stick around as the manager. But cheerleading is not as easy as it looks. A lot of girls don't make it past the first round."

"We'll just see about that, won't we?" said Alex. "Now I'm thinking I might just try out and see how it goes."

"Awesome!" squealed Emily.

Everyone went back to talking and eating. But Alex's mind was in a whirl. What had she just done?

# CHAPTER THREE

"You did what?" asked Ava, her eyes round with disbelief.

"I told them I was going to try out," said Alex miserably. "I know. It was dumb. I just sort of blurted it out without really thinking about it."

The girls were home from Sal's, getting ready for bed in the bathroom they shared. Their Australian shepherd, Moxy, had splayed herself out right in front of the door in the hallway. Ava could hear Tommy playing his keyboard in his room, and their parents had gone to bed early. Coach had been pretty quiet and preoccupied after the Tigers' loss.

Ava put some toothpaste on her toothbrush

and frowned. "Alex, you do realize you're going to get cut immediately. No offense, but these girls are really good. They've been practicing for years. They go to cheer camp and stuff in the summer. And this is Texas. You've probably noticed that people don't do things halfway here."

"I know," said Alex. "But Rosa practically forced me to say I'd go to the first day of tryouts. It was a matter of pride. My pride." She sighed dramatically. "All I have to do is make it past the first round of cuts and then I'll be done. I can prove to her that I'm not a total klutz, and Emily says after I demonstrate my commitment to the sport, the coach might let me be manager for the team, which will be an easy way to fulfill my athletic requirement."

Ava nodded, but it was hard to hide the exasperation she was feeling. Alex was always getting into these situations by saying stuff without thinking about it. *Well, there's nothing I can do,* Ava thought. Her sister would just have to get knocked down and learn her lesson.

Ava spat into the sink and rinsed her mouth. "I'm going to bed, Al," she said. "I have a big game tomorrow."

"Do you mind very much if I don't go?" asked

Alex. "They posted the video of the routine we have to learn for Sunday, and I think I'm going to need all day tomorrow to practice it."

Ava nodded. "That's fine. You never know what's going on in the game anyway." With a wry grin, she headed into her room and left her sister in the bathroom, practicing clapping her hands with enthusiasm.

The middle school Tiger Cubs' game didn't go well either. Ava's team lost 17–7. The car ride home from the game was a quiet one.

"It's nice that you went in as wide receiver," said Mrs. Sackett, breaking the silence at last.

Ava shrugged. "I didn't touch the ball the whole game," she said. "Except to kick that extra point."

"But it's great that Coach Kenerson had enough confidence in you to put you in," said Mrs. Sackett. "Right, Michael?"

Coach flicked a glance at Ava in the rearview mirror. "That's right, Ave," he said. "You ran a nice pattern."

Ava sighed and gazed out the window at the

passing landscape. "I heard Mr. and Mrs. Kelly grumbling to Andy after the game," she said. "I think they were mad Coach K pulled him and put me in. They probably thought we could've won if he'd stayed in the game." The Kellys and their nephew Andy Baker had been some of Ava's biggest opponents in her quest to be the first girl to play football in Ashland

Coach sighed quietly and shook his head, as he turned the car into the Sacketts' driveway. "Doug Kelly means well," he said. "He's just looking out for his nephew. But the fact is, the Armadillos were the better team. I don't think it would have made a difference one bit. You're not as skilled yet as Andy Baker, but you're faster and have great instincts. It was just a tough outing for Corey, and our linemen didn't give him enough protection."

After a long shower, Ava felt much better. She put on comfy sweatpants and a T-shirt and headed to Alex's room to see how she was doing with her cheer routine.

"Hey," said Alex, although the word came out in the form of a grunt.

"How's it going?" asked Ava, suppressing a grin as she watched her sister attempting a split.

Alex groaned and fell over to the side in an ungainly tumble. "Ow!" she said. She pounded lightly all over her thighs with her fists. "I can't unclench my muscles." She groaned again. "I'm not even close to doing a split. I'm, like, a foot off the floor!"

"It takes time to get to that level of flexibility," said Ava, coming into the room and sitting on the ground next to her sister. "Have you really stretched out first? You don't want to hurt yourself."

"Sort of," muttered Alex. "But I've seen you do one before. You don't even warm up first."

"Al, I stretch all the time, though," said Ava. "Here, I'll show you some stretches you can do."

The two of them spent the next fifteen minutes in a series of floor positions.

"Try one," said Alex. "Try doing a split and let me see how far down you can go."

Ava hesitated. She didn't want her sister to feel bad. But she took off her sneakers, and in her socks, lowered herself down on the polished wood floor, in the space between the rug and the wall, and slowly descended into a full split. She pretended to wince with discomfort a little, but in fact, she was good at splits and could drop into one pretty readily.

"You can totally do one!" marveled Alex. "That's so awesome!"

"You can too," said Ava encouragingly. "You just need to practice every day."

"I don't have every day," said Alex. "I have to do one by tomorrow." She sighed. "Hey, remember back when we were in ballet class when we were, like, five? You were the best one in the class. It was only when you learned you had to wear a pink tutu that you flat-out refused to go back. Remember that?"

Ava rolled her eyes and chuckled. "Guess we haven't changed all that much," she said.

"Can I show you the video of the routine I'm supposed to learn?" asked Alex. "Maybe you can help me with it, just a little?"

Ava smiled. "Let me just eat something first. I'm starving. We can practice down in the living room."

Half an hour later, both girls stood side by side in front of Alex's laptop, which they had propped up on a high shelf of the curio cabinet. They had moved most of the furniture into a corner of the room and rolled up the rug so they could work on the bare wood floor.

"Okay," said Ava. "Let's try it one more time. Together. Right foot first. Knees high. Arms go straight up and out in a V. Ready?"

Alex nodded resolutely as the music began, her face the picture of concentration.

Ava counted along. ". . . five, six, seven, eight! March-march-arm-arm-clasp, turn, head-head, squat-two, three, four . . . jump!"

Ava looked behind her to see if Alex had sprung up in unison with her. Alex was sprawled on the rug, a dejected look on her face. She'd fallen. Again. Ava groaned inwardly. This seemed hopeless.

Someone in the doorway clapped, and the girls turned. It was Tommy.

"Not funny, Tommy," said Alex through gritted teeth. She scrambled to her feet.

"No, really, you guys looked great, at least for a minute," said Tommy. "Is this for a talent show or something?"

"Al's trying out for cheerleading tomorrow," explained Ava. She was slightly out of breath. They'd just practiced the routine four times in a row, and Alex had goofed on some part of it each time.

"Al's trying out . . . for cheerleading?" repeated Tommy, looking from one girl to the other with a look of surprise.

"Yes!" said Alex defiantly. "Why is that such a shock?"

"Oh, no, I didn't mean that," said Tommy quickly. "You'll be awesome."

"No, I won't," sighed Alex. "Ava's so much better than I am, and I've been practicing this dumb routine all morning. She got it the first time through!"

"Well, maybe she can wear a wig and go as you!" said Tom with a grin. "You'll be fine. Just don't drop anyone on her head, okay, Al?" He drummed a comical *buh-duh-bum!* rhythm on the doorjamb and left.

"Okay," Ava said, turning back to Alex. "Let's try this one more—" She stopped.

Alex was staring at her with a thoughtful expression.

"No," said Ava firmly. "Whatever it is, no."

Alex was still looking at her, but then her gaze drifted upward, and she stared hazily into the middle distance, somewhere over Ava's head.

Ava knew that look. Her sister was formulating a plan. And Ava felt a growing sense of unease. "Al. I mean it. It would never work. Not in a million years." But she could see it was no use. Alex's eyes were beginning to sparkle deviously.

# CHAPTER FOUR

Alex and Ava hadn't switched places with each other in years. Ava recalled trying it on their mother a few times—little things, like when they were six and Ava wanted a third cookie. She tried to pretend she was Alex and asked for one. Or the times they'd tried switching places at the dinner table. Mrs. Sackett always seemed to know. Sometimes it had worked on their dad, but he usually figured it out after a few minutes. Although they'd talked about doing it many times, they'd never swapped roles with each other in a situation that counted, out in the real world.

"I have no clue how to be a cheerleader," said

Ava. She was still exhausted from practicing the routine, but now she wondered whether her elevated heart rate was caused less by the dance routine and more by anxiety at what her sister was proposing.

"You're ten times better at it than I am, and you know it. Plus, you don't have to make the team. You just have to get past first cuts so I can prove to Rosa that I can do it."

Ava started to raise the point that it would prove nothing if Ava made the cut, rather than Alex. But she stopped herself. She knew from experience that Alex tended to adopt her own brand of logic in situations like this. She tried a different approach.

"We don't look a thing alike."

Alex scoffed. "We're identical twins, Ave. The emphasis being on the word 'identical.'"

"What about our hair? Mine's short, yours is long. It won't work. Case closed."

"Case reopened. Remember that fake ponytail hairpiece Mom bought me two years ago when I was Princess Leia from *Star Wars* for Halloween? I still have it! Remember how she pulled together two-thirds of my hair and made a circle braid on one side and then attached that ponytail to the other third of my hair and coiled it into another circle braid on the other side?" She got a dreamy look on her face. "I looked awesome."

"I refuse." Ava put her hands on her hips. "Let the record show: I'm not going to wear my hair like Princess Leia."

"You don't have to, silly! But your hair is long enough that I can attach the fake ponytail to the back of your hair, and then we can smooth the rest into place with hair gel and tons of bobby pins, and it will look perfect. Just like mine."

Ava could feel her resolve weakening. She had learned through experience that when Alex got like this, with that determined look in her eye, it was pretty much useless to resist. "It's never going to work," she muttered.

Alex bounded over and gave her a huge hug. "Thanks, Ave. You're the best sister ever."

"This is never going to work," said Ava for what felt like the millionth time in the past twenty-four hours.

Alex looked up and managed, with some

effort, not to laugh. Her sister was standing at the door of Alex's room, dressed as though she were on her way to a basketball practice. Alex moved toward her twin and guided her into the room, closing the door quietly. *This is going to require some delicate diplomacy,* Alex thought.

"Of course it will work, Ava," she said. "But first of all, we need to work on the outfit."

"What's wrong with my outfit?" asked Ava.

"Well, let's start with the shorts. Those are for basketball. They're long and baggy—totally wrong for cheering. Here, try these."

She picked up a pair of neatly folded shorts from her dresser and handed them over.

Ava stared at the shorts. "Please tell me these are just the underwear."

"No, they're the shorts you need to wear. They're snug-fitting so you can kick and stretch and stuff. Put them on."

Ava stepped out of her basketball shorts and shimmied into the shorts Alex had given her.

"Good. Stop looking at me like that. Now we just need to fold down the waistband. Like this." She moved around her sister, flipping down the waistband, and then tugging the shorts down a bit so they were sitting on Ava's hips. "That's how they wear them."

Ava seemed speechless with horror, but Alex kept talking brightly. "And you can't wear that baggy Patriots tee, Ave. You look like you, and we're trying to make you look like me. Here, put this on." She handed Ava a stylish, fitted periwinkle-blue athletic shirt with a V-neck.

"Also, you can't wear basketball high-tops," said Alex. She picked up her bright-blue cross trainers, which she'd bought for their fashion rather than their function. She hadn't ever actually cross trained in them.

Ava stared at them. "Really?"

"Really. I couldn't ask Mom to invest in real cheerleading shoes just for tryouts, especially because I'm not going to make the team. But these are better than your high-tops—those are a dead giveaway that you're you, not me."

Reluctantly, Ava bent down and untied her high-tops.

"Now you look awesome!" said Alex, when Ava stood before her in Alex's clothes and shoes. "Let's start on the hair and makeup."

"Makeup?" Ava looked at her, stricken.

"Of course, makeup! It will be subtle. But

you have to look like me, remember?"

She guided her sister over to her vanity table and pushed her gently down onto the padded bench. Then she got to work.

First Alex tackled Ava's hair. The false ponytail looked pretty good, once she'd smoothed back the front of Ava's hair with hair gel and lots of bobby pins. Then she set to work applying foundation, concealer, blush, shadow, liner, mascara. . . .

Ava was not good at sitting still. As Alex approached her with the eyelash curler, she recoiled as though her sister were brandishing an instrument of torture.

"What's that thing?" she croaked.

"It doesn't hurt," said Alex. "It just curls your lashes. Trust me."

"I don't trust you."

"Well, sit still anyway. I'm almost done."

Ava whimpered quietly as Alex finally finished with her makeup. Then she took a step back and surveyed her sister's face with a critical look.

"It's pretty good," she pronounced. "You look like me."

Ava darted a wary look in the mirror. "I look totally ridiculous."

"No, you don't."

"And my lips are sticking together."

"You just have to get used to lip gloss. Now I need to get a bow for your ponytail, to cover up the place where it's attached. That's what cheerleaders wear: big bows. I'll be right back. I think we have one in the Christmas decorations box. Don't go away."

"Where would I go, looking like this?" Ava asked her own reflection in the mirror. Then a movement behind her made her swivel around. Tommy was standing in the doorway.

His mouth dropped open. From the look on his face, Ava could tell he wasn't fooled by all the makeup she was wearing—he knew she was Ava.

Ava sprang up and pulled him into the room, closing the door behind him. "You can't tell," she said.

Tommy seemed to have lost the power of speech for the moment. He was goggling at her. At last he spoke. "What are you guys up to?"

"I couldn't say no to her," said Ava, her gaze dropping to the floor. Her glossed lips felt sticky, and her eyes itched, but she didn't dare touch them with all the mascara she had on. "She asked for help with tryouts today."

"Ha!" he laughed. "So you're going to go as Alex and try out for the cheer squad?" Tommy seemed mesmerized by Ava's transformation. He walked a complete circle around her, shaking his head in amazement.

Alex returned with the bow and didn't notice Tommy at first. "It doesn't quite match what you have on, but I think if we—" She stopped when she saw Tommy. "Oh," she said quietly. "Hi. Don't tell."

"What if she makes it?" asked Tommy.

"She isn't going to," said Alex quickly. "She just has to get past the first round of cuts today. Then I'll go tomorrow and get cut." She explained to Tommy, briefly, how Rosa had challenged her. "But it's not just to show Rosa," she added quickly. "Evidently Coach Jen only considers taking a manager who tried out and got cut. She wants someone with a real commitment to the sport. So my plan is to get cut and ask to be the manager. It's an easy way to fulfill my athletic requirement. And I'll get to hang out with all my friends."

Tommy folded his arms and looked from one girl to the other with narrowed eyes. "And just how do you propose getting to school without Mom or Coach seeing you?"

The girls exchanged a look. Neither of them had really thought about this. Of course, they could walk—it was just a little over two miles. *But what if we run into someone we know?* Ava thought.

Alex gave Tommy a pleading look. "Will you drive us? Please?"

Tommy grinned wryly. "Okay. Mom and Coach are in the kitchen. I'll go tell them I'm willing to drive you guys. You should go out through the front door. But Al, you better put on something of Ava's. You look too much like you. Not that Mom and Dad will be fooled if they see you—but other people might be."

"Right! Good point!" said Alex. "I'll go put on a football jersey of Ava's."

Ava couldn't help grinning, despite her frazzled nerves. This would be something to see.

"All right. I'll go down now. Give me a couple of minutes to get them talking, and then head to the car."

The plan worked. Alex returned, having tucked her long hair up into a battered old Celtics hat she'd found in Ava's room and put on a Patriots jersey. She and Ava tiptoed down the stairs and around to the side, where they sat in the car, waiting for Tommy.

"Mom better not come out here," muttered Ava, tugging at the hem of her too-tight shirt. She took out her phone and used the camera to examine her shadowed, mascaraed eyes. "She'll know in half a second we're not who we say we are." She surveyed her sister. "I wonder if Charlie would be able to tell if he saw us. Then he would."

"Oh! That reminds me," said Alex briskly. "Try to work into the conversation that I—you—I mean you, Alex, have broken up with Charlie."

"And when am I supposed to casually work that into the conversation?" asked Ava. "Between backflips?"

"Just try to mention it, and if anyone asks you why, just say 'it's complicated' and look like this"—Alex rolled her eyes upward, crumpled up her chin, and made her lower lip tremble, the picture of heartbreak—"and then change the subject."

"And why have I—you—broken up with him, just out of curiosity?" asked Ava.

"Because I think Corey and Lindsey might like each other again, and there's no danger of him asking me out twice, which might make Lindsey upset."

Ava's temples were beginning to throb. She would never remember all this.

"And also," Alex continued, "as you and I both know, I'm a really bad liar. I keep forgetting what I've told people and acting clueless when they bring something up I forgot I said. People keep mentioning Charlie and I keep saying, 'Charlie who?' and I just want to stop lying to people. It isn't right, and it's exhausting."

"Yes, because what we're doing right now is perfectly moral," said Ava drily.

"This is different," said Alex. "We're not lying to people outright. We're just switching places for a day."

Ava realized that Alex actually thought her reasoning was logical. Her twin was excellent at rationalizing.

"Here comes Tommy," said Alex. "Get down, quick. Mom is waving to us from the window." She waved quickly at their mother and then pulled down the brim of her Celtics cap.

A few minutes later they were on their way to the middle school.

Tommy kept looking in the rearview mirror at

Ava and stealing sidelong glances at Alex. "This is kind of freaking me out, you guys," he said.

"It's freaking me out too," said Ava, as they pulled into the school parking lot. "What are you going to do during the clinic?" she asked Alex.

"I'll watch as much as I can," said Alex. "So when you make first cuts, I'll know what to expect at tryouts tomorrow. But I need to do it on the sly. I'm supposed to be you, and you would never sit in the stands and watch. There's no way you could stay still that long."

Tommy nodded in agreement as he stopped the car, then turned and grinned at them. "Good luck, Ava-I-mean-Alex. Be great. But not too great."

"Thanks," said Ava.

She and Alex joined the groups of girls heading into the school. "Remember," whispered Alex, "smile a lot. Laugh at what people say. Gossip with my friends. Talk about my favorite TV shows and bands. You know, just be me!"

A wave of anxiety shot up and down Ava's spine as her sister gave her arm an encouraging squeeze.

"I'll be with you in spirit!" whispered Alex, as Ava followed the rest of the group into the gym. "Good luck!"

# CHAPTER FIVE

Alex watched her sister walk into the gym, which was crowded with girls trying out, along with parents, high school cheerleaders, and a couple of coaches standing with clipboards. She realized the taller one must be Coach Jen.

"Alex! Over here!" called a girl standing near the bleachers.

It was Emily. She was standing with Lindsey and Rosa. Alex started to wave back and then remembered she was Ava. Close one! She watched Ava join her friends and could tell by the way they were gesturing that they were telling Ava how cute she looked. "Smile, Ave!" whispered Alex under her breath. She couldn't tell whether Ava was smiling.

Stepping out of the doorway, Alex hurried down the dim corridor. She'd go to one of the side entrances of the gym, which opened behind the bleachers, so she could spy on the clinic without being noticed.

"Alex! Over here!"

Ava almost didn't look in that direction, but then remembered she was supposed to be Alex. Emily was beckoning to her. She was standing with Lindsey and another girl—was her name Rosa? She should have gone over all the names with Alex ahead of time. One more flaw in a series of flaws that made up this very bad plan. She walked over, remembering to smile. She felt her bow swivel a little and readjusted it. All she needed was to have her fake ponytail fall off.

"You look adorable!" squealed Emily, and Lindsey smiled at her. Rosa stopped looking around the gym for a moment to nod.

"Thanks," said Ava. And then, remembering she was Alex, "So do you! I love that, um, shirt. Those glinting sparkly things are awesome."

"We were just talking about *Saturday Central* last night. Did you watch it?" asked Lindsey.

Ava knew enough to know that was a popular comedy show, although she rarely watched it with Alex. She tried to remember whether Alex had watched it last night, but Ava had been down in the study, watching film with Coach until pretty late. She went for the noncommittal response. "Oh! Ah! Ha-ha!" she said.

"I know, right?" Lindsey said, evidently taking that for a yes. "And wasn't Director Peal totally, like, amazing?"

"Director Peal?" repeated Ava. "Um, I think I missed that part. Does he have a new film?" Emily and Lindsey stared at her blankly.

"Direct Appeal?" prompted Emily. "That new band that you are crazy about? Didn't you say you have a total crush on Nigel?"

"Oh! Oh, right!" said Ava. She could feel beads of sweat breaking out on her upper lip and hoped her makeup wouldn't streak. "Right. I totally have a crush on Nigel. Don't tell Charlie!" Then she remembered Alex's instruction. "Except maybe you should, because we just broke up!" She resisted the urge to cover her face with her palms, remembering how much bronzer she was wearing. This scheme was never going to work.

Lindsey and Emily looked shocked.

"Oh, Alex! You and Charlie broke up? I'm so sorry!" said Emily. "What happened?"

"It's . . . complicated," croaked Ava miserably. An image flashed in her mind of the expression Alex had demonstrated—she had looked like she was suffering from indigestion. Ava just couldn't bring herself to try it. And besides, she, Ava, really did have a sort-of boyfriend named Charlie. So how could Alex expect her to pretend to be Alex, pretending to have a boyfriend named Charlie, pretending to have broken up with him? The upside-down-and-backward situation felt like one of those books about time travel that always made Ava's head swim.

It was Rosa who changed the subject, and Ava silently thanked her.

"So I talked with Sam last night."

Ava knew Sam Haskins was one of the eighth-grade captains.

"She said first we're going to run through the routine from the video in small groups," Rosa said. "And then we learn a cheer, a new dance routine, and a jump sequence." She turned to Ava.

"How's your pike? Have you been working on it?"

Ava had no idea what a pike was. "It's pretty good," she replied.

"Good, because I heard Molly over there has improved a lot since cheer camp last summer, even though she sprained her ankle at the end of it." Rosa gestured toward a small girl with reddish hair who was sitting in the stands with her leg propped up in front of her. "Did you go to cheer camp back in Massachusetts?"

Rosa was starting to annoy her. Ava knew she could be competitive, but there were certain people—like Rosa—who seemed to bring this out in her more, and Ava could feel herself getting increasingly worked up by the second. "No," she said flatly. "But I've been doing some practicing on my own." That was true. She'd spent the morning watching cheerleading how-to videos online and practicing along with them.

"Oh. Well, I know you want to make first cuts," said Rosa. "Good luck!" she added sweetly.

Ava suddenly realized she was wearing her most competitive expression, one that Tommy always said could make stone statues quake at the knees. She quickly put on a more Alex-like smile, but inside, she was getting fired up for this clinic. She was going to prove to Rosa, and everyone, that Alex could do this. Even if she was Ava.

Luckily, just then Coach Jen clapped her hands and called everyone over to start stretching.

Alex peered through the railings at the side of the bleachers. She had a pretty good vantage point to observe what was going on. She watched Ava chatting with Lindsey and Rosa and Emily. It looked like she was doing okay. Then she heard Coach Jen clap her hands and call the group over.

Alex was too far away to hear what Coach Jen was saying to the girls, but the talk was brief, and soon the eighth-grade captains were leading the group through a series of stretches. Coach Jen and her assistant stood to one side, talking with each other and consulting the clipboard. The high school girls stood in a small group, chatting and laughing.

Next the girls were divided into three groups. Alex could see that the coach for Ava's group was Kylie's older sister. What was her name?

Yvette! That was it. Alex watched the groups practice the cheer they'd been asked to learn for the clinic. She yawned. Ava was doing great. She looked like one of the more coordinated girls out there. *Still,* Alex thought, *is it really necessary that I observe the whole afternoon?* If her sister did make first cuts, and Alex had to come back for practice tomorrow, she was sure Ava could teach her the routines. She found a cozy-looking niche in a corner where some exercise mats were stacked, sat down, and pulled out *A Tale of Two Cities*, which she was reading for her advanced English class.

# CHAPTER SIX

Two hours passed quickly. Alex finished a chapter, put away her book, and went back to her lookout post to see what was going on. Everyone was lining up for the final routine. The coaches and high school cheerleaders were sitting in the bleachers, watching. Where was Ava?

Alex spotted her, second from the left. It was a little eerie, how much Ava looked like her at that moment. Her ponytail was still pinned securely in place, although Alex noted that Ava had flipped up the waistband on her shorts. Oh well—Alex had asked a lot of her. At least she was remembering to smile.

The music started. The girls began the dance.

It was an upbeat, popular song, one that you couldn't resist dancing to when you heard it. Alex moved her feet as she watched the girls step, step, step, twirl. Check mark left, check mark right, V-pose. Then a mambo-cha-cha-cha, turn around, and do it again. Ava was excellent. Alex marveled at how confidently she nailed every step. She bounced up and down with excitement. And was it her imagination, or was Rosa glaring at Ava out of the corner of her eye?

After the routine, she watched the girls demonstrate jumps. Ava did a hurdle, a pike, and a toe touch. She was awesome at all three.

Tommy picked them up right at five o'clock, at the side door of the gym.

"How'd it go?" he asked them, as Alex slid into the front seat and Ava into the back. Ava had called shotgun, but Alex argued it was more believable that she—pretending to be Ava— would be sitting in the front.

Alex noticed that Ava's face was flushed and her eyes were shining. She knew that look. Her sister loved competing, no matter what the sport.

"I thought she looked fantastic," said Alex. She turned toward Ava. "How do you think you did?"

"Well, except for the fact that my mouth is paralyzed into a permanent frozen smile, I think it went pretty well," said Ava. "They're posting the results online at seven tonight."

Tommy was shaking his head. "I can't believe you guys got away with this. You're so lucky Mom and Coach didn't offer to come get you. They were in the middle of interviewing Luke."

"Who's Luke?" asked Alex.

"Luke Grabowski. He's my friend who's applying for the tutoring job in the Sackett household, remember?"

"Oh yeah. My tutor," muttered Ava. "I'm really looking forward to that happening." The Sacketts had recently found out that Ava had ADHD, and they were trying to find someone to help her with homework a few nights a week.

They parked in the driveway. "I'll go in and make sure they're still with Luke," said Tommy. "You two might want to switch back before you go inside. You know Mom won't be fooled for a second by your getups."

Alex knew he was right. As soon as he'd gone inside, she unpinned Ava's fake ponytail and pulled the Celtics cap off her own head. Her long curls tumbled down around her shoulders. The girls swapped shirts, which wasn't pleasant for Alex, as the shirt of hers Ava had worn was damp with sweat. "Ew," she said, curling her lip and plucking the shirt away from her body.

"What did you expect?" said Ava. "Cheerleading is hard work."

Alex watched Ava pull out several bobby pins and then try to mess up her own hair.

"It's not doing what it usually does," said Ava. "You put too much hair spray in it."

"Here," said Alex, thrusting the Celtics cap toward her sister. "Put this on."

"Good plan," said Ava. "And hand me a tissue so I can wipe some of this gunk off my face."

Ava followed her sister inside. Moxy came bounding around the corner to greet them, and then skidded to a stop and cocked her head to one side, looking perplexed.

"I think she's confused because our clothes must smell like both of us together," whispered Ava, giving Moxy a reassuring pat on the head.

Moxy's tail thumped on the floor, but without the usual enthusiasm.

There were voices coming from the study. She exchanged a quick look with Alex. They silently agreed it would be better to say hello briefly than try to sneak past their parents. Anyway, they were now more or less back to their regular selves.

"Ava!" called Coach. "Come meet Luke."

"You too, Alex," said their mom.

The girls both stopped at the door of the study.

A blond boy about Tommy's age stood up from his chair and turned toward the door. He seemed nice enough, Ava thought. And he had a friendly smile. But she was still nervous about having a tutor.

"Hi," she said shyly, stepping into the room.

"Hi, Ava," he said.

"Yo, dude!" said Tommy from the hallway. "Have you bamboozled them into thinking you're an upstanding citizen?"

Luke blushed and rolled his eyes, which Ava thought was sweet. She already felt a little bit better about having to work on her homework with him.

"Ignore Tom, please," said Coach. "This is Ava's twin sister, Alex." He gestured to Alex, who was in the doorway. "How were tryouts, Al?"

When Alex didn't answer immediately, Ava turned to look at her sister. Uh-oh.

Alex's mouth had dropped open, and her head was tilted slightly to one side. *If this were a cartoon,* Ava thought, *Alex's eyes would have hearts for pupils.* Ava knew this look. Her sister was love struck.

"Hey, Al?" prompted Coach. "Tryouts? Did they go okay?"

Alex seemed to snap out of it. "Tryouts? What tryouts?" She tore her gaze away from Luke and focused on Coach. "Oh! Tryouts! Yes! They were great! Awesome!"

Mrs. Sackett narrowed her eyes at Alex.

"Well, it was nice to meet you," Ava said to Luke hastily, and hustled her sister out of the room before their mom could examine either of them too closely.

Ava shoved her sister kindly but firmly into Alex's room with a whispered "Go change!" and then hurried toward her own room. The sooner she got into the shower to wash the spray out of her hair and the rest of the gunk off her face, the better.

She was gathering up clean clothes in a bundle to take to the bathroom when she heard Tommy call her from down the hall.

"Hey," she said, stopping at the door of his room.

"Hey," he said, and beckoned her in. "I've got a little situation I need some help with."

Ava came in and sat down on his bed.

"You look really freaky with makeup on," he said.

"Thanks. That's what you called me in to tell me?"

"No. Sorry." Tommy got up and quietly closed the door. "It's about Friday night and the game."

"It's going to be a close one, huh?" said Ava.

"Yeah, and that's the thing," said Tommy. "See, I know I'm not going to get into the game. PJ's not going to come out when it's that tight a contest. And Dion's getting healthier every day, and he's ahead of me. And the thing is, I have somewhere I would rather be than standing on the sidelines, knowing there's no chance I'll get into the game."

"Where?" asked Ava, although she had a feeling she already knew the answer.

He looked at her directly. "The tri-school band competition. It starts at eight p.m., and I want to be there."

Ava nodded. She was silent. This was touchy. Coach would never say yes to Tommy leaving the game midway through. It just wasn't what you did as a member of a team, no matter how important—or unimportant—you were to the team's chance of winning. But Tommy would definitely need to leave at halftime if he wanted to get to the concert on time.

"You realize Coach would kill you if you left."

"Gee, thanks. Like that hadn't occurred to me."

"Sorry."

"Can you help me think of something?"

Ava pondered. "Maybe you could pretend to be sick."

Her brother shook his head. "I thought of that. But he'd never believe it. He knows how tough I am."

Ava raised her eyebrows. "Aren't we being modest?"

"No, I mean, we all are. All the guys understand

you need to be semi-comatose or bleeding from multiple wounds before you're allowed to admit you don't feel well. It's the football culture."

"Not if you suddenly come down with a stomach bug," Ava pointed out. "Even Coach would send you away. No one on the team would want you within half a mile of the locker room for fear of catching it."

Tommy stroked his chin thoughtfully. "Hmm."

"Go to him at halftime. Tell him you have a stomach thing. That you think you caught it from someone at school. Tell him you don't want to infect the rest of the team." As soon as Ava had said it, she felt a shudder of unease at how easily the lie had come to her. *Am I becoming a hardened criminal? One who can come up with diabolical schemes without batting an eye?*

"I think you're onto something, Ave. I can bolt at halftime," said Tommy, with growing enthusiasm. "I can get a friend to drive me—if I hop into a waiting getaway car, I should get to the concert in plenty of time. We're third on the program." Tommy looked intrigued. Then his face fell. "But the band competition might run late. What if I'm not home before Coach is? If I'm supposed to be half-dead of the stomach flu, I can't be out when he gets home."

"Good point," said Ava. "I'm not sure." She and Tommy sat side by side on Tommy's bed, their chins resting on the heels of their hands, brooding.

Ava sat up. "It's highly unlikely he'll be home right after the game. He always has to stay and talk to the press and get interviewed and stuff. But on the off chance that he gets home first, I can tell him you got a friend to drive you to the walk-in clinic. Like Luke or somebody. On whom, by the way, Alex already has a mega-crush."

Tommy rolled his eyes. "I could've seen that one coming," he said. "I always forget how dreamy Luke is. I guess I don't stare into his eyes as often as I should. But yeah, Ave, I think this plan might just work. Have I told you you're awesome?"

"No."

"Well, you're . . . wait. Forget it. You're not awesome."

"Why not? What's wrong with this plan?"

"Uh, hello? What about Mom? If she hears I'm sick, she'll be home to check on me in four minutes flat. She'll have me rushed to the nearest hospital."

"She won't hear. Who would she hear from? You say something to Coach at halftime. You leave. No one would go running into the stands to tell her."

"What about after the game, though? Coach will tell her then, and she'll go straight home to cook up some strengthening broth for me."

"Ha! No, she won't!" said Ava triumphantly, leaping up. "I just remembered! She told me she has an old friend coming in from out of town Friday night. She's having a late dinner with her, leaving straight from the game. So you're clear! She won't even see Coach until much later."

"Ave?"

"Yep?"

"You're awesome."

"I know."

"But you do still look freaky with that eye stuff on. And you have glitter on your nose. Go wash your face."

"Thanks," she said drily, getting to her feet. "I will."

As she headed for the bathroom, she found herself wondering how, in just two days, she had become partners in crime with both of her siblings.

# CHAPTER SEVEN

Ava came down to dinner half an hour later, having scrubbed her face with a washcloth and washed her hair twice to get all the hair spray out. She stepped over Moxy, who was sprawled as usual across the kitchen floor, and slid into her seat.

Coach was talking about the upcoming game on Friday. "They're deep and talented on both sides of the ball. Defensively, their corners are fast and athletic, and offensively, their line protects their QB very well. It's going to be a close game." He took a moody bite of his meat loaf. "PJ's going to have his work cut out for him. He's going to need your moral support big-time, Tom."

Tommy flicked a glance at Ava. She held his gaze for a fraction of a second and looked down at her plate. They both knew that what Coach was saying was code for *You're not going to play and we all know it.*

"So tell us all about tryouts, Alex!" said Mrs. Sackett, who seemed eager to change the subject.

"Tryouts?" said Alex. "Ow! Oh, oh, right. Tryouts. They were great." She smiled.

Ava, who had just kicked her sister under the table, was surprised that Alex didn't seem more upset about lying to their parents, even if she wasn't great at it. Was her sister heading straight to a life in a penitentiary? In English, Ava's class was reading a story by Edgar Allan Poe called "The Tell-Tale Heart." Although usually Ava had a hard time sticking with a story for very long, this one had held her attention. It was about a guy who'd murdered someone and stuck him under the floorboards, but then the guy went mad and imagined he heard the pounding of his victim's heartbeat growing louder and louder until he couldn't stand it anymore and turned himself in to the police. Was guilt not pounding through Alex's brain like it was through Ava's?

"Was Molly Clifford there?" asked Mrs. Sackett.

"I ran into her mom at the grocery store, and she told me Molly had sprained her ankle, but I'm not sure how bad it was."

Alex blinked. "Molly? Oh! Yes. She was. I mean, no. I don't think so. I mean, I can't remember."

On second thought, Ava realized, Alex was a terrible liar. She jumped in to rescue her sister.

"I think you mean she was there but wasn't actually trying out," said Ava hastily. "What I heard was that Molly is under doctor's orders to stay off her ankle for two more days, so they're going to give her a tryout on Tuesday."

"Oh, right," said Alex. "I forgot."

Ava could feel her mother shift in her seat. She didn't dare look up. Her mom was nearly impossible to deceive.

"What's that you're wearing, Ava?" Mrs. Sackett asked suddenly.

Ava froze. Had she somehow left the bow in her hair or something?

Her mom put a hand on Ava's cheek and pulled it gently in her direction. "Your eyes. Are you wearing glitter? There's some on your cheek, too."

Ava felt her whole face go hot. She'd had

no idea how to get all the stupid glitter off her face. She'd scrubbed every inch of herself, of course, but it just seemed to transfer bits of glitter from one part of her body to another. She heard Tommy snort across the table, and if she could have been sure exactly where his legs were, she would have planted an indignant kick to his shins.

For once, Alex saved the day. "I was experimenting on Ava," she said.

Coach raised one eyebrow and inspected Ava's face with interest. "Huh," he said.

"And by the way," Alex continued, "are you guys planning to hire Tommy's friend? Was his name Luke?"

"We're not sure yet," said her mother. "We've just started the process of interviewing people, and we're not totally sure what we're doing, but he certainly seemed bright, and enthusiastic. And more than competent."

"And dreamy," coughed Tommy into his napkin. "Ow!" he said loudly. "Who kicked me?"

Alex must have been sure exactly where Tommy's legs were.

# CHAPTER EIGHT

As soon as they were finished helping with the dinner dishes, Alex nodded to Ava, and the two girls hurried upstairs and into Alex's room. They sat side by side as Alex's fingers flew across the keyboard. A moment later they were staring at the list of girls asked to return for the second day of tryouts.

Ava let out a whoop. "We made it!" she yelled, doing a fist pump and then giving Alex a high five.

Alex laughed. "You made it, you mean. You were so good, Ave. I cannot wait to see Rosa's face when she has to admit that I can do anything I set my mind to. Or, er, that I set your mind to."

Both girls looked at each other with troubled expressions. Alex was starting to feel that her circular logic wasn't quite working. What was she proving here? And now that she was past the first round of cuts, the consequences of what she and Ava had done were finally starting to sink in. She'd been so focused on just "making first cuts" that she hadn't really thought beyond this point. *How did I not contemplate the next step?* she thought.

"Well, anyway, it's done," said Ava, getting to her feet. "I'm glad I could help you out, but I'm really relieved not to have to do this again."

"Um, about that," said Alex slowly.

Ava's eyes narrowed. "Alex," she said. "No."

"Sit down," said Alex gently. "Let's discuss this calmly and rationally."

"Al, there's nothing to discuss. I did what you wanted. You made first cuts. You go tomorrow and you don't make the team. Then you can be manager or whatever."

Alex shook her head, slowly, wearily. "No, Ave, it won't work. First of all, if I go to try-outs tomorrow and I am completely and utterly horrible, when I was amazing the day before, they're going to suspect something. I don't know the routines you learned today. The clinic went on for hours, and I didn't watch each and every minute, to be honest. And there's no time for me to learn them!" With a pang of guilt, she thought about how she'd curled up on the mats and read for most of the clinic.

"So e-mail Coach Jen and tell her you had second thoughts, and that you've decided to quit."

"I can't do that, Ave! If I quit now, she'll never in a million years let me be manager. You of all people know that coaches do not look kindly on quitters. If I don't become manager, I'm looking at some horror show of a sports activity. Like Square Dance Club!" She shuddered. "No, I have to get cut fair and square, but it has to be you. You have to go back and just be convincingly semi-awful, rather than a disaster, which is what I would be."

Ava shook her head violently back and forth. "Al! Tomorrow is Monday. I have football practice. I can't miss football practice to go to cheerleading tryouts!"

"Don't worry," said Alex. "I have a plan for that."

Ava stared at her with a disbelieving look.

"Just tell Coach K that you have a doctor's

appointment. Kids do have doctors' appointments sometimes. He'll be fine with that. Please?"

Ava opened her mouth to say something, and then closed it again when she saw the desperate look in her sister's eyes. She sat, massaging her temples. Then she said, "Okay. You're right. Even though I thought—and still think—this whole plan was stupid and doomed, I see that what you're saying makes some sense, in a warped kind of way. We're in this too far. If you show up tomorrow and you don't know anything, they'll guess in two seconds that we switched places and we'll both be in big trouble. But you know if Mom finds out about this, she'll kill us both."

"I know." Alex hugged her. "Ave, thanks. You're the best, most generous sister anyone could ever ask for."

"But no glitter this time," said Ava firmly.

"Hey," said Kylie in a low voice. She and Ava were sitting side by side in social studies the next day. Kylie nudged Ava's sneaker under the desk with the side of her green cowboy boot. "You are definitely distracted today. You keep drumming your fingers, tapping your foot, squirming in your chair, and you just used the blue pencil to color Panama, and blue is our ocean color."

Ava stared down at their map of Central America and groaned. "Sorry," she said. She picked up the eraser and scrubbed at the blue.

"What's up? You seem to have a lot on your mind today."

"I guess I am a little distracted," said Ava. She chuckled ruefully. "Maybe it's my ADHD." *Or maybe I'm distracted because I'm helping both my sister and my brother with their harebrained, risky plans to deceive people,* she thought.

"How's tutoring going?"

"It hasn't started yet, but I think my parents might have found someone. And my sister promptly developed a crush on him," said Ava.

Kylie rolled her eyes. "Of course she did. Hey, you know what you need? Some riding therapy! Maybe you should come to the ranch this weekend and we'll take the horses out for a nice, long ride."

"That sounds awesome," agreed Ava. "But first I have to get through the rest of this week."

Monday afternoon, just after the last bell rang, Ava hurried to her football teammate Xander's locker, which wasn't far from hers.

"Hey, Xander," she said, as he slammed his locker door closed and hoisted his practice stuff onto his shoulder.

"Hey," he said. "What's up?"

"I need you to tell Coach K I won't be at practice today."

"Are you sick?" he asked her, raising his eyebrows.

Ava gave a little cough. "Just a little. It's more that I have a really bad sore throat and my mom thinks it could be strep, so I'm going to get a strep test. I don't want to infect the team."

"Okay," he said. "Feel better." He headed down the hallway toward the locker room.

Ava blew out a breath. *Getting out of going to practice wasn't so hard,* she thought. She hurried off to meet Alex.

They had picked a remote bathroom in a far corner of the school, where almost no one went at this time of day. Alex was already dressed in

Ava-wear. Her hair was tucked into the Celtics cap, and she had on one of Ava's faded, comfy T-shirts and jeans.

"Freakishly convincing," said Ava, when she saw her sister. "Except I don't wear bubblegum-pink lip gloss. You need to wipe it off."

Alex's hand flew to her mouth. "Right. I forgot. Let me borrow your lip balm."

Ava dug it out of her pocket and handed it over.

"We need to hurry," said Alex, getting right down to work. "Tryouts are in fifteen minutes."

Ava sighed and took the neatly folded T-shirt and shorts from her sister. "This is crazy," she muttered as she went into the stall to change.

Ten minutes later Ava looked at herself in the mirror and saw her amazed reflection staring back. Her eyes looked huge, rimmed with dark, smudgy eye pencil. Her lips glistened with pink gloss. She gave her hair a shake, and the fake ponytail swayed back and forth. She had to admit that once in a while she missed the feeling of having long hair. Although this big bow did look ridiculous.

"Four minutes till tryouts start," said Alex briskly, moving to open the door. "Remember: Don't try too hard. Be below average. Don't get carried away and get all competitive, okay? Just be bad enough to get cut, and it will all be over."

"It will all be over," repeated Ava, and hustled off toward the gym.

There were fewer girls in the gym today, of course, but still at least twenty. Ava was put into a different group from the day before, led by a high school girl named Serena. Rosa was also in the group. After stretching, they practiced poses.

Serena demonstrated something called a scorpion. Ava watched in amazement as Serena stood on her left foot and used one hand to grab her right foot, bent at the knee, behind her. Slowly and smoothly, her right foot went up, up, up behind her body, until it was at the back of her head. Then she grabbed the leg with her other hand and stood perfectly balanced.

"Wow," the girls said.

"This is a flexibility pose," said Serena, lowering her foot. "I'll spot you guys, don't worry."

A few of the girls were super flexible, and although not as graceful as Serena, could do the pose with some guidance. When it was Rosa's turn, she expertly grabbed her foot and sinuously moved it up until she looked just like Serena.

Ava was next. "I've never tried this," she admitted to Serena under her breath.

"Don't worry. I'm here to spot you," said Serena reassuringly. "I know you're flexible, but don't push yourself too hard."

Ava had no trouble grabbing her back foot. Up, up it went.

"Nice!" said Serena encouragingly. "Now reach back as far as you can with your other hand and grab your foot with both."

Ava was amazed. She could grab her foot with two hands!

"Nice flexibility!" said Serena. "Have you really never tried this before? You're doing great!"

With a start, Ava reminded herself she was supposed to be performing badly today. No, no! Not great. She dropped her foot quickly. "Oops," she said. "Lost my balance." She smiled apologetically at Serena and rejoined the group.

# CHAPTER NINE

"Ava! Hi! Ava? Hello?"

With a start, Alex realized Corey was addressing her. She jumped back from where she was peering through the slats in the bleachers at Ava's tryout. Corey was clearly just back from football practice: He was carrying his practice pads and had black stuff on his cheeks.

"Oh, hi," she said, adjusting the brim of her Celtics hat. She touched the back of her head and tucked a stray tendril of long hair underneath the cap.

"How are you feeling?"

"Fine. Why?"

Corey looked puzzled. "Xander said you had an appointment."

"Oh! Oh, yeah, fine. It was just a dentist appointment, a routine checkup."

Corey looked even more confused. "He said you thought you might have strep."

"Oh! Ah, ha-ha. Well, my dentist is awesome. He was a double major in dentistry and medicine and he, ah, he . . ." Alex desperately needed to change the subject. "Anyway, I don't have strep—or any cavities."

"That's good," said Corey uncertainly. "So how's Alex doing with tryouts? I heard she was pretty good yesterday."

"Yeah, she made first cuts," said Alex, unable to contain the pride in her voice. "She doesn't think she's good enough to actually make the team, because she has too many other interests and can't commit to such a specialized skill, but she's a determined person and believes you can accomplish anything you set your mind to. And she decided she really wanted to make first cuts."

"Huh. No kidding." He studied her curiously. "Well, I need to run. My mom's waiting for me. See you at practice tomorrow."

"Yep, see you."

He turned. "In case you were wondering, practice was pretty tough today. We did a lot of conditioning. But Coach K said we're watching film tomorrow. He says we need a day to regroup and rest up. So no pads."

"Okay, thanks," said Alex, stopping herself just before she said, *I'll let Ava know.*

Corey paused again. "Hey, do you remember the name of our fake extra-point call?"

Alex could only shake her head. She had no idea what he was talking about.

Corey nodded. "That's okay. I can ask Xander." He started to walk away.

Was he looking at her suspiciously? Had he guessed that she wasn't really Ava?

Then Corey said, "What's up, Alex?"

Alex felt an electric jolt through her body. How had he recognized her through her disguise? They didn't know each other that well. Then she heard Ava respond behind her.

"Hey, Corey."

Oh. So he'd been saying hi to Ava, dressed as Alex, who had come up behind her. Alex wiped her brow. They both watched Corey disappear down the hallway.

"I need to go wash my face and take off this dumb bow," muttered Ava in Alex's ear.

"You'll have to wait till we get home," Alex whispered back. "There's nowhere to go without risking being discovered."

"Okay, but I can't be seen on the bus," said Ava. "I'm supposed to have strep. Let's walk."

They slipped out of a side door and set off for home.

"So how did it go today? Did you remember to be bad?"

"Um, yeah," said Ava. "Mostly."

Alex noted a hint of uncertainty in her tone.

"I landed funny on a jump and turned my ankle a little," said Ava. "But I think it'll be okay for practice tomorrow. Football practice, I mean, of course."

"And they'll make final cuts tonight?"

"No, they said one more day of tryouts, because there are quite a few girls who could go one way or the other, and Molly gets to try out tomorrow."

Alex stopped. "Ave, then you have to go back tomorrow. You can't not show up."

"Yes, I can," said Ava. "I am not going to miss another day of football practice."

Alex remembered what Corey had said, and a desperate idea popped into her head. "I'll go to football in your place!"

Now it was Ava's turn to stop walking. "Alex. Do you realize what you're saying?"

"No! I mean, yes!"

"You wouldn't know the difference between a tight end and a split end if your life depended on it."

"I know. I know. But Corey told me—you— that tomorrow Coach K is just talking to the team. There's no actual practice involved. So I can be you, because I don't have to do anything except sit there and watch films and listen to the coaches talk."

"Hey, Ava! Think fast!" came a voice from behind them.

Both girls whirled around. A basketball came sailing out of thin air, headed straight for Alex. The twins hadn't realized they were so close to home already—they were passing the little park near their house, and Jack was shooting baskets on the court.

Alex gave a little squeal and covered her face with her arms. The ball bounced off her elbow and rolled away.

"Alex!" hissed Ava under her breath. "You're me, remember? I would have caught that! Now go get the ball!"

Alex ran over and picked up the ball. "Hey, Jack!" she called. "Didn't see you."

"Hey," Jack yelled back. "Let's see what you've got, Ave! From there!"

"What's he asking me?" Alex hissed at Ava

"He wants you to try a long bomb from here. Shoot the ball. Into the basket."

"From here?"

"It's just a game. Jack and I do it all the time. Go on."

Alex dribbled the ball once, then hoisted it into the air, her elbows flapping out awkwardly. It missed the basket. It missed the basketball court. It landed in the grass near the play area and bumped to a stop against the slide.

Ava closed her eyes with a pained expression.

Jack looked at Alex-as-Ava with a surprised look. "Nice shot," he said. "Not."

"Ha-ha! My bad!" called Alex. Ava tugged her by the sleeve, and the two girls hurried off.

# CHAPTER TEN

The next day Alex sat in the girls' locker room, lacing up Ava's cleats. She had to admit, Ava's clothes certainly were comfy. Her baggy T-shirt, faded and soft from dozens of washings, flopped over her loose shorts, which billowed around Alex's legs and extended almost down to her knees.

"Hi, Ava," said a girl as she entered the bank of lockers where Alex was sitting. "No pads today?"

Alex shook her head. "Nope. We're watching film."

The girl, whom Alex didn't know, was quickly changing into what looked like volleyball clothes.

Alex admired the way her mahogany-brown hair tumbled over her pretty purple shirt as she propped a foot up on the bench to tie her shoe.

"That burgundy tee is a perfect complement to your hair color," she blurted out.

The girl looked at her, startled. "Huh?" she said.

Shoot. *Ava would never say anything like that,* Alex thought. "Nothing," she said. "I better get going—see you!"

The girl cocked her head at Alex, looking slightly confused, but managed a "Yeah, see you," as Alex hurried out to practice.

One of the coaches—was it Coach D'Annolfo?—was standing outside the locker rooms, directing kids down the hall to an empty classroom to watch the film. Alex slipped into the darkened room and found a seat way at the back, without looking at anyone.

"Sackett! Feeling better?" barked Coach Kenerson from the front of the room, where he was fiddling with a camera attached to a laptop.

Alex froze. What would Ava say? "Yes, Coach!" she said, and prayed he wouldn't ask her anything else.

"You missed the pro formation review we did

at practice yesterday, Sackett. Tell me: Where would the X receiver line up?" he asked.

Wait. He was asking her? Fear clutched her heart. Ava had been right. It was a terrible, terrible idea for her to go to Ava's football practice. Alex's heart pounded like the big bass drum in the high school marching band.

"Did you say the X receiver?" she stammered, stalling for time. "I—uh—"

Wait. Was someone saying something to her? Someone was. Corey. He was sitting right next to her and talking in a low voice.

". . . to the left, to the left, to the left," he murmured.

"To the left!" she blurted out.

Corey was still murmuring, "The X receiver would align to the left of the formation, on the outside."

"The X receiver would align to the left of the formation, on the outside," repeated Alex, in a louder voice.

Corey murmured, ". . . and the X receiver would be on the ball."

"And the X receiver would be on the ball," she added.

"Good! Nice job, Sackett," said Coach

Kenerson. He hit the play button and rolled the film.

Alex nearly wept with relief. She collapsed in her seat, her heart still hammering so loud she was sure the whole room could hear it. She turned to Corey and whispered, "Thanks."

He gave her a sideways smile and an almost imperceptible nod, and leaned back in his chair to watch the film.

"Okay, don't get mad, but I think you're Alex, not Ava," said Corey, as they walked toward the locker rooms. The "chalk and talk" session was over, and Coach K had dismissed them for the afternoon, urging them to get a good night's sleep. Most of the guys had run ahead, laughing and jostling one another.

Alex had finally allowed herself to relax the tiniest bit because the official football stuff was over, but now she felt a jolt throughout her whole body. She darted a look at Corey. She thought about protesting, but that would be futile. He knew. And anyway, he'd saved her life in there, answering Coach K's question.

"Yes," she whispered. "Please, please, please don't tell."

"Why would I tell?" he asked with a grin. "Was that you I was talking to yesterday, watching the cheer tryouts and pretending to be Ava?"

Alex nodded ever so briefly, her eyes darting from side to side, making sure no one was listening.

"So Ava's trying out for cheerleading, pretending to be you." Corey gave a low whistle. "That's bold."

"It's really complicated," said Alex out of the side of her mouth. "I can explain, but maybe not here, or now."

Coach D'Annolfo and Coach MacDonald walked past them, discussing something on a clipboard.

After they'd passed, Corey shrugged. "No need to explain. I'm sure you guys have your reasons. Will you . . . ah . . . will Ava be at football practice tomorrow?"

Alex nodded vigorously.

"Okay, good. Tell her to text me and I'll fill her in on what we went over today."

Alex smiled gratefully at him as he headed into the boys' locker room. He was a good guy.

Of course, she no longer *like* liked him, but she could still admire the fact that he was a good guy. And trustworthy—hopefully.

Alex went straight to the gym to watch the end of the final day of cheerleading tryouts. She sat in the bleachers, and besides one mom who was sitting with two younger kids, overseeing their homework, she was the only spectator. Ava and five other girls were practicing a dance routine in a small group.

Rosa, Molly, and Emily were together in another group. Lindsey was in yet another group, along with Annelise and some other girls Alex didn't know.

Alex frowned. Ava was not looking at all terrible. She was moving in sync with Yvette as the high schooler led them through the steps. In fact, she looked like she was the most coordinated in the group. Alex sighed. Her sister was so competitive. She couldn't not try her hardest. Well, she'd better not have done this well all day. What a disaster it would be if Ava made the team! Alex shuddered, just thinking about it. As she looked at the group of girls working together with such skill and coordination, she couldn't even begin to imagine herself out there. She'd fall over her own feet. They practically looked professional—and there were still cuts to be made!

"Hey, Ava," said someone to her left.

It was Jack Valdeavano. He must have come in through the side door behind the bleachers and was standing alongside them, surveying the scene. Alex smiled at him. "Hey, Jack."

"I promised my aunt I'd stop in to see how Lindz is doing," said Jack. He and Lindsey Davis were cousins. "Aunt Beth says Lindsey tells her absolutely nothing, so she has to resort to spying. I've been drafted into the Secret Service."

Alex laughed. "It looks like Lindsey's doing great," she said. She self-consciously touched her hat, making sure her hair was still tucked up and under.

"Plus, I figured you'd be here," he added, his face getting a tiny bit pink.

For a second Alex panicked. Why was Jack turning pink talking to her? Aside from the fact that she knew she looked cute in this Celtics hat? And then she remembered she was Ava. He was talking to Ava, not to her. What would Ava say here? Alex wondered. Probably nothing. She'd probably punch him in the arm or something.

But he was definitely blushing. *Ha!* she thought. *So he does like Ava!* She sat up a bit straighter and swiveled her body so that her knees were pointing slightly in his direction. She'd read somewhere how important body language was in sending someone a message. Crossing your arms and legs sent a message that you weren't open to what a person had to say. Open arms, a slight lean in the person's direction—those were little signals that told the person you were interested in him. After all Ava had done for her, she owed it to her sister not to mess up here. Jack was supercute. Ava could do much worse.

"Hey, listen." Jack didn't look at her. He kept his eyes fixed on the girls working through the routine. "I was wondering."

Alex waited with bated breath. Was he going to ask her—Ava—out? She gave him a small, encouraging nod.

"Do you want to, like, hang out together after the game on Friday night?" He said it quickly, all in a rush, still not looking at her. His face went two shades deeper pink.

She knew it! He was asking her out! Ava would probably make a joke out of this and change the subject, or tell him to stop being such a dork, or grab his hat and toss it behind the pile of mats or something.

But she wasn't Ava. She just looked like Ava. Still, she had better seek clarification.

"So you mean, like, a date?" she asked.

He looked taken aback, and momentarily at a loss for words. "Oh! I, ah, yeah. Yes, I guess you could call it a date. But just to Sal's. And there's probably going to be a lot of guys there and we don't have to—"

"I'd love to!" she interrupted him.

He closed his mouth. Then he grinned at her with a slightly surprised look in his eyes. "Cool!" he said. "I'll come find you after the game then."

He darted away, and Alex leaned back and smiled with satisfaction as she thought about how much easier it was to talk to a guy she didn't have a crush on. And Ava was going to be so pleased with her. Really, this identity switch was proving to have some real side benefits.

# CHAPTER ELEVEN

Ava was hot and sweaty and totally sore, but she still felt exhilarated. Cheerleading was really fun! It wasn't exactly a contact sport the way football was, but there was a lot of teamwork and real athleticism involved. These past few days had given her a newfound respect for how coordinated and highly trained a cheerleader needed to be.

"So how terrible were you?" Alex asked her in a low voice. They were on the late bus home, still in disguise, sitting close to the front, where there were empty seats all around them. Most kids preferred to sit toward the back.

Ava hesitated. "I tried. I wouldn't say I was

terrible, but I wasn't great or anything," she said. "I intentionally didn't jump very high on my hurdle or my pike."

"Do you think you'll be cut?"

Ava pressed her lips together uneasily. She was worried about this. She hadn't paid a lot of attention to how the other girls were doing. It was hard to compare yourself when you were trying to learn a complicated routine. "I think so. I hope so. There were some really talented girls, like Rosa and Lindsey. And there were some girls there who really, really want to be on the team and have clearly put in a lot of practice. It makes me feel terrible that I could be keeping someone off the team who deserves it."

Alex shook her head. "You won't be, if you get cut. There are several girls vying for just the few slots. Not all of them will make it. You haven't deprived anyone."

"Well, there's also Molly, who still has a sprained ankle. She was there today, participating for the first time, and her ankle was pretty heavily taped. She did okay but was clearly not a hundred percent. This isn't a game, Al. It's pretty stressful to think I might be bumping some deserving girl off the squad. I better get cut."

They rode in silence for a while. Then Alex said, "Corey knows."

Ava turned to her, eyes wide.

Alex explained how Corey had jumped in and saved her from Coach K's question. And how he'd guessed she wasn't Ava but had promised he wouldn't tell anyone.

Ava got a creepy-crawly feeling along her spine. This was getting more and more complicated. She liked Corey. He wasn't the kind of guy who would go around telling everyone, but still. It would be a huge disaster if her football teammates found out she had tried out for cheerleading, even if she was pretending to be her sister! She groaned softly.

"Anyway," said Alex briskly, "tomorrow it will be over. They'll post cuts first thing in the morning, and I'll be off the team and can go to Coach Jen and ask to be manager. And you can go to football and we can pretend it never happened. We got away with it, Ave. I can't tell you how grateful I am that you were willing to do this for me."

Ava managed a small smile.

"Oh, and one more thing," Alex added mischievously. "I'll need to help you with your outfit for the game Friday night."

"Why?" asked Ava, immediately growing suspicious. "What's happening Friday night?"

"Well, you'll want to look extra nice for your date."

"My what?"

"Your date. With Jack."

"My what?!" Ava shouted the words. She felt her face get hot as a few kids on the bus turned to look at her curiously. In a quieter, but no less frantic voice, she hissed, "My what?!"

"Your. Date. With. Jack." Alex said it slowly, as though Ava didn't understand English very well. "He asked you out. And you said yes." She smiled at Ava encouragingly. "I know, I know. There are some things I'm just smoother at than you, so isn't it great that I was pretending to be you when this happened? There's definitely an upside to this whole thing."

Ava was momentarily speechless. She could only stare at her sister in disbelief. She and Jack liked each other, that was clear. But she was not ready to think about him as boyfriend material. There was Charlie, for one thing. Sure, she'd been considering telling Charlie that she really just wanted to be friends. But she hadn't yet. And what if going on a date with Jack wrecked the fun relationship they had? He was more of a buddy than a romantic interest. She groaned and sank down low in her seat.

On Wednesday morning the twins raced toward the girls' locker room before school started. The list was posted on the bulletin board just outside. A clump of girls was already there, so they had to wait before they could get close enough to see the list. Some were looking thrilled. More than a few looked like they were about to cry.

"Madison Jackson must not have made it," Alex whispered to Ava, as Madison walked past them dejectedly.

Ava nodded grimly.

Finally Alex and Ava were able to step up to the posted sheet. They stood side by side, scanning the names.

Alex saw her own name first, but she couldn't get her brain to compute. "Wait," she said. "If my name is on the list, does that mean I was cut or that I made it?"

Ava made a little fist pump upon seeing Alex's name, but almost immediately seemed to regret having done so. A stricken look appeared on her face. "Al, it means we made it." She pointed to the note at the top of the sheet:

The following girls should report to cheerleading practice today, Wednesday, at three fifteen p.m. Thank you to everyone who tried out.—Coach Jen

Alex was still having trouble absorbing this information. "Wait. When you say I made the team, do you mean, I made the team?" She looked at Ava reproachfully. "This wasn't supposed to happen, Ava. What did you do? Execute a back aerial or something?"

Ava started to retort, but several more girls were crowding in to have a look at the list. So she pulled Alex back a few steps, out of earshot.

"I'm sorry. I tried. It isn't easy to flub up on purpose. You'll have to tell Coach Jen you can't do it," said Ava.

Alex shook her head. "Not after all this. I can't.

Why would I go through three days of tryouts and then quit? You just have to go back today."

"Al, you know I'm not going to do that. You're on the team now. You either do your best or you tell the coach you're quitting. You'll just have to figure this out," said Ava.

And Alex could see that she meant it. This time, there would be no talking her into it. Ava cared too much about football to miss another real practice. Besides, she was right. What good would it do if Ava showed up today? There would be tomorrow, and the next day, and the next day. At some point, Alex was either going to have to start going to practice, or she would need to quit.

"Congratulations, Alex!" said a girl passing them.

Alex smiled weakly. "Thanks." She was struggling not to reproach Ava for being so competitive. Couldn't she have been a little less good, for once? But knowing Ava, Alex should have realized this would happen. This was a disaster. A horrifying realization dawned on her. "There's a pep rally last period on Friday," she said. "What am I going to do? I have no idea how to do the routine!"

"Go to practice today and learn it," said

Ava, and she headed away to class.

Alex stared after her sister. Ever since she'd told Ava about the date with Jack that she'd said yes to, Ava had seemed very irritable with her. Really, Alex was the one who had the right to be mad at her. This was all so wrong.

At cheerleading practice that afternoon, Alex joined Lindsey, Emily, and Rosa for stretching.

"We're going to be so awesome!" squealed Emily excitedly as she stretched out her long legs in front of her and bent over to effortlessly touch her nose to her knees.

Alex tried that too. She couldn't get within ten inches of her knees. She tried the stretch Lindsey was doing, which looked slightly more manageable. One leg bent in a half cross-legged position, the other crossed over it, her body turned to one side. Wait. How did this work? She was getting it all wrong. She stretched out her triceps instead, which was much easier. You just pointed an elbow up alongside one ear and pulled it gently with the other hand.

"I was a little afraid Molly might make it

instead of you, Alex," said Lindsey in a low voice. "She still gets a day more to try out, but I don't think she's totally back to normal. Coach told my mom that if Molly's good enough, we'll just have one extra girl on the squad. But I don't think she's anywhere near as flexible as you are. Maybe she can try again in the spring."

Alex looked over at Molly, who was sprawled out in a split. She gulped as she watched Molly bend her head over her knee and touch it with her nose. She was as graceful as a swan. Alex redoubled her efforts at stretching out her triceps.

"How's your ankle, by the way?" asked Emily.

"My ankle? Fine. Why?" asked Alex.

"Um, because you said it was bothering you yesterday," prompted Emily. "After you landed on it funny?"

"Oh, yes, right," said Alex weakly. "It's better."

Coach Jen called the team over and practice began.

On the late bus home, Ava tried to console Alex. "You can't have been that terrible, Al."

"Oh, Ava! I was beyond terrible!" moaned Alex. "I was a catastrophe! I didn't know any of the routines! I had no clue what anyone was talking about! Coach Jen just looked dismayed every time she looked at me. I almost dropped a girl when I was supposed to lace my fingers together and then boost her up onto Emily's knee!"

Ava grimaced. "So what happened?"

"I told Emily and Lindsey I'm going to quit."

"Smart."

"But they talked me out of it."

"They—they talked you out of it? How?"

"They said that everyone has an off day, and that I've got too much talent to quit. They made me realize that the team needs me. And Molly wasn't very good either. Emily and Lindsey said so themselves. They said maybe she'll be okay when her ankle heals, but that I'm bigger and stronger than she is so they can use me to spot until I'm 'back to my old self.'" For the last part she crooked her fingers in air quotes.

"What if you tell Coach Jen your ankle is too sore? She knows I landed on it funny the other day. You can tell her it's bothering you and ask if you can be the manager."

"I think she already has a manager. She picked Ariel Salina, who got cut on the second day. So if I don't stay on the team, I'll have to do some other sport instead!" She buried her face in her hands.

"Maybe you weren't as bad as you thought," said Ava uncertainly.

Alex lifted her head out of her hands. She'd brightened considerably. "Do you think so?"

"Um, well . . . " To be honest, Ava didn't think so. She was just trying to cheer Alex up. Chances were Alex had been worse than she thought.

"Because that's what Emily and Lindsey told me, too!" Alex said eagerly. "Maybe I wasn't as bad as I thought!"

Ava's heart sank. Alex was so willing to take people at face value. She doubted Emily and Lindsey had really meant what they'd said to Alex, any more than she'd meant what she'd said.

"And Coach Jen must not think I'm all that awful, because she assigned me to be a spotter for the pep rally," Alex continued. "I guess I'm pretty strong for my size. Or, well, you are. But how badly could I mess up spotting?"

Ava grimaced. "Well, Al, as Tommy pointed out, it's kind of important not to drop someone on her head."

Alex laughed. "I think I can handle it, Ave."

Later that evening Ava and Tommy reviewed the plan for Friday night.

"So I'll meet you outside the locker room as soon as halftime starts," said Ava. "I'll have your bag of concert stuff ready for you."

"Good," said Tommy. "And Luke says he'll be waiting to take me to the concert. Mom's definitely going out with her friend, so that part's all set."

"Did she tell you who her friend was?" asked Ava. "Because she was kind of mysterious with me about it."

"Just a friend from back in Massachusetts who's in town for the night, was all she said," said Tommy with a shrug. "She said it was someone passing through on her way somewhere else."

That reminded Ava about Charlie. She needed to figure out what to do about him. Should she tell him about Jack? Or just let things . . . fade out naturally?

Her phone buzzed with a text from Jack. Was that fate speaking to her? She felt her face get warm and hoped Tommy wouldn't notice.

Of course Tommy noticed. He raised one eyebrow. "Need to reply to that, Ave? Don't let me stop you."

She flushed deeper. "Guess I better," she said, and left the room.

# CHAPTER TWELVE

Alex swallowed hard and braced herself. It was Thursday afternoon, at practice, and Annelise, the flier, stood above Alex's head. One of her feet was in Lindsey's intertwined hands, the other foot was in Rosa's. Her arms were up in a high V. Alex was the back spotter. Emily was the front spotter.

Coach Jen was counting them through the high stunt called an extension prep. ". . . Five, six, seven, eight!"

Lindsey and Rosa hoisted Annelise up into the air. She twirled once around, her body taut, her arms clasped to her chest, and then bounced down into the girls' waiting arms. Alex caught her from behind, and together they lowered her feetfirst to the floor.

"Nice, girls," said Coach Jen. "Let's do it one more time."

Alex reapplied her lip balm from the tube Ava had loaned her. As Coach Jen began the count, she hastily shoved it into the tiny pocket of her shorts and braced herself to spot Annelise again.

". . . Five, six, seven, eight!" The two bases and two spotters clapped, turned, and hoisted Annelise.

"One, two, three, four, five, six, seven, eight!"

Up she went in a high V, and then dipped down.

"One, two, three, four, five, six, seven, eight!"

Up she went, spun, and—

"Eeee!" shrieked Rosa, as all of a sudden she toppled to the ground.

In slow motion, Alex saw Annelise spin once in the air, and wobble lopsidedly where Rosa was no longer standing.

Alex lunged to the side and threw her body underneath the spinning girl, who fell down to the floor on top of her. Alex's chin hit the ground hard and Annelise landed mostly on Alex's back and upper thighs. She felt a sharp pain radiate from her chin to all her nerve endings.

Alex saw spots in front of her eyes. The pain in her chin was considerable, but she couldn't reach up to feel for damage because her arms were pinned underneath Annelise, who was still lying on top of her.

There was a great deal of commotion as Annelise was lifted off her, and Alex was helped to her feet. She could see a small crimson smear on the floor where her chin had been.

"Oh my gosh, she's bleeding!" Alex heard Emily say with a gasp.

Rosa was on the floor, wailing. "I slipped! I'm sorry! My foot just flew out from under me!"

Alex glanced down at the floor, hoping against hope that she wasn't going to see it. But there it was. The tube of lip balm. She must have dropped it in her haste to recap it, and Rosa must have slipped on it.

People were crowding around her, but she managed to kick the tube out of the way. It bounced and rolled behind the heavy gym curtain divider.

"Is Alex okay?" Alex heard Annelise ask through the crowd.

"She cut her chin," said Lindsey.

"Are you okay?" she heard Emily ask.

"I'm fine!" said Annelise. "I landed completely on Alex, though! What about Rosa?"

"She's okay," Alex heard Sam say, as though through a fog.

Coach Jen pushed her way through the group and gently cocked Alex's head back a little bit so she could look at her chin. She pursed her lips. "Your chin is cut pretty badly," she said. "This is going to need stitches."

Stitches! Alex had never had stitches in her life. Ava had had them multiple times, thanks to all her sports and her daredevil climbing and bike riding. But not Alex—she was always the careful, deliberate one. "I can call my mom," said Alex in a small voice.

Mrs. Sackett was at the school in fifteen minutes, a smear of paint on her chin and still wearing the blue-and-white-striped apron from her pottery studio. On the way to the walk-in clinic, she called their pediatrician's office. On speakerphone Alex heard the nurse say they'd call ahead to the walk-in clinic.

Coach Jen had bandaged Alex's chin with gauze and tape. It hurt, but the waves of guilt washing over her made Alex feel so much worse. She had caused the accident! This was all her fault. Her mom kept glancing anxiously at her as they drove to the clinic, one hand on Alex's knee.

At the walk-in clinic, they were seen almost immediately by a nurse, who examined Alex's chin. She asked Mrs. Sackett a bunch of questions and wrote everything down on a clipboard, and then hurried out. A moment later the doctor walked in. Her name was Dr. Kumar. She was young and nice, and told Alex everything she was going to do before she did it. The numbing shots hurt a little at first, but after that, the stitching part was just a disconcerting tugging. At last Dr. Kumar finished and taped Alex's chin with a surprisingly small sticky bandage. Then Dr. Kumar asked Alex a bunch of questions, shone a light into her eyes, and made her go through a series of exercises like extending her arms out and touching her nose, first with one index finger, then with the other.

"I think we can rule out a concussion," Dr. Kumar told Mrs. Sackett, patting Alex on the back. "But keep an eye on her, and be sure to call if you have any concerns. She can visit her regular doctor in a week to have the stitches removed." She handed Mrs. Sackett an information sheet about how to care for Alex's stitches, and another about concussions.

Mrs. Sackett thanked Dr. Kumar, and after the doctor had left, helped Alex collect her things.

"I'm going to keep you home from school tomorrow," she said to Alex. "Even though the doctor doesn't think there's much danger of a concussion, I'd rather play it safe and keep an eye on you for a day."

Alex started to protest. That would mean she'd miss the pep rally at school! But as she thought about it, she liked her mom's plan more and more. How could she face her teammates? She stared down at her T-shirt, which had three dark drops of blood on it.

As they drove home, her mind flashed back to what had happened. Rosa slipping. Annelise falling. She, Alex, diving headfirst underneath Annelise in order to cushion her fall. The whole thing had been Alex's fault. Rosa had slipped on Alex's lip balm, for sure. On top of the gnawing guilt she was feeling, Alex was also acutely aware of another, darker voice, telling her that if this was the worst thing that had happened, she was very lucky. She had no business being on the team. How could she have thought she would be good enough to be an Ashland cheerleader? She could have caused someone a serious injury.

When they got home, Alex told her mother she was going upstairs to bed.

# CHAPTER THIRTEEN

On Friday Alex stayed in bed as she heard Ava getting ready for school. Her mom had, as usual, been right. Her chin did hurt, her stitches itched, and she didn't want to face everyone at the pep rally.

She made it through a dozen of her vocabulary flash cards, finished the English reading through the following Wednesday, and worked on some sample math problems. After lunch she watched a documentary about termites from an African country called Burkina, although her heart wasn't in it. She couldn't stop thinking about what a terrible thing she'd done.

By early afternoon, she came to a decision.

She went downstairs to the kitchen, where her mom was paying bills at the table.

"Mom, could you drive me to school?"

Her mom frowned. "I'm not sure that's a great idea. The school day is almost over. What's the point?"

"I need to talk to Coach Jen. My chin is fine. It's really important that I do this. I want to set something straight. Please, Mom? The rally starts at two thirty, and it's over by the end of the school day."

Mrs. Sackett stood up. "Okay, honey. If it's important to you, I'll bring you to school."

Alex hugged her. Sometimes her mom just seemed to understand.

Ten minutes later Alex knocked softly on the open door of the English department office. Coach Jen was also a sixth-grade English teacher. By a stroke of luck, she was the only teacher in the office. She was grading a stack of papers.

"Alex!" said Coach Jen, standing up and coming around her desk. "How are you, you poor thing?"

"Hi, Coach," said Alex. "I'm okay. I got three stitches. My jaw hurts a little, but other than that, it's not so bad. Can I talk to you for a minute?"

Coach Jen's eyes flicked to the clock above the doorway. "The rally starts in twenty minutes, and I should go check on the team soon, but sure, if we make it brief." She pulled up a chair for Alex. "Sit."

"Is Annelise okay?"

"She's fine. A little bruise on her elbow, but you bore the brunt of the fall. Rosa feels terrible about slipping. She says she stepped on something and just went down."

Alex's memory flashed back again to Rosa going down and Annelise tumbling. She stared down at the floor. "Coach Jen," she said in a tiny voice, "it was my fault Rosa slipped."

Coach Jen crossed her arms and cocked an eyebrow. "You were nowhere near her, Alex."

"I dropped my tube of lip stuff. And she slipped on it."

Coach Jen pursed her lips. "Ah," she said. "Well, it was an accident."

"No, but it's worse than that," said Alex. "I shouldn't be on the team at all. I'm terrible."

"Well, ah, you started out strong, Alex. Those

first three days of tryouts, you looked like you deserved to be out there, but then—"

"Coach. There's something else I really need to tell you."

Coach Jen folded her hands in her lap and waited.

"I did something really bad. Those first three days of tryouts? When I was so good? That wasn't me. It was my identical twin. She and I switched places and she tried out, pretending to be me."

Coach Jen's eyes widened ever so slightly, but she said nothing and allowed Alex to continue.

"But it wasn't my sister's idea at all. I'm the one who should get into trouble, not Ava. She just went along with my plan. See, I wanted to make the first round so badly. But then I planned to get cut and no one would be worse off. Plenty of girls made the first round, so it wouldn't be like I was keeping someone off the team."

Alex paused. She waited for Coach Jen to say something, to yell, to pick up the phone and call the juvenile detention center. But she just sat there quietly and waited for Alex go on.

In a rush, Alex finished blurting out her confession. "But then everything went really wrong when Ava was too good, and she made it. I should have told you right then and there, but, well, I really wanted to be part of the group. And I thought—I thought maybe I could do it. Which was crazy, because I stink." She hung her head, her cut chin starting to throb. "I'm really, truly sorry. Please let Molly take my place. I don't deserve to be on the team. I'll go apologize to them and tell them the whole story, even though they're all going to hate my guts and—"

"Alex."

"—I'll probably lose my class presidency and maybe even get suspended. And—"

"Alex?"

"And I totally understand why I shouldn't be the assistant manager or the assistant to the assistant manager, but—"

"Alex! Stop," said Coach Jen.

Alex closed her mouth. She waited for Coach Jen to start yelling.

"You're right, Alex, that what you did was very wrong. But I think you've already punished yourself enough. And I do believe you've learned a valuable lesson."

"Crime doesn't pay," Alex said seriously.

The corners of Coach Jen's mouth twitched a little, and she nodded. "And I agree that you forfeited any right to be a manager, even if I did have a position available for you, which I don't."

Alex swallowed down the lump in her throat and fought back the tears of shame that were welling up in her eyes.

"I'm sorry about your injury, Alex. But it could have been so very much worse. You took a big risk not only with yourself, but with others. I shudder to think what could have happened. I do think you need to tell Rosa that the incident wasn't her fault, because she feels terrible about the whole thing."

Alex nodded miserably. Of course it had to be Rosa. Rosa would tell the whole world, and Alex would be shunned for the rest of her middle school career. She didn't even deserve to be in the Square Dance Club, after all that had happened.

"But I think we can leave it there," said Coach Jen. "I don't think there's any value in sharing the whole story with everyone. But Alex?"

"Yes?" said Alex in a tiny voice.

"Maybe don't be so hard on yourself all the time. You don't have to be good at every single thing. You're good at enough!"

Alex nodded. "Thanks, Coach Jen. I'll try. And

I think I learned another lesson: Maybe I should be a little less quick to open my big mouth and make promises I can't keep?"

Coach Jen chuckled. "Maybe, Alex. Now I need to go to the rally. I'll speak to Molly about a permanent spot on the team. She was already going to fill in for you today."

Alex smiled with relief. "Thank you," she said, and she meant it.

"Why don't you come along? You can tell the team your decision."

The squad was in the locker room, getting dressed in their uniforms, when Alex and Coach Jen appeared in the doorway together. The pep rally was due to start in ten minutes.

"Girls," said Coach Jen. "Alex has something to say to you."

Something in her tone must have told the girls it was serious, because they all stopped what they were doing and turned to listen.

Alex stared down at her shoes and cleared her throat. She was more nervous than she'd been before her presidential candidate speech in front of the entire school. "Guys, I came to apologize to you."

Now the girls were so quiet you could hear

the ticking of the clock above the door.

Alex took a deep breath and went on. "I was the reason Rosa slipped. I dropped my lip balm on the floor. And I haven't been—um—myself the last few days. I don't think I'm cut out for cheerleading, after all. I told Coach Jen that I'm resigning from the team."

Alex saw Lindsey and Emily exchange a shocked look.

"I'm especially sorry to Annelise, for almost dropping her on her head. And to Molly, for almost taking her place on the team even though she deserved it. And to Rosa, because she slipped on the lip balm that I dropped. I wasn't paying enough attention to Coach Jen and I was careless." She looked up at them. "So, well, sorry again," she said, and walked out of the room without looking back.

She'd asked her mom to wait for her in the car, and now Alex hopped in and buckled her seat belt in silence. Her mom didn't ask her anything. She seemed to sense that she should leave Alex alone. They drove home without speaking.

Once back, Alex headed up to her room, closed the door, and buried her face in her pillow. She stayed that way for a while. She wondered if her parents could afford boarding school. Or reform school. Or a study abroad program that started the following week. She wondered if seventh graders were allowed to join the military, or the Peace Corps. She had to go somewhere, because she couldn't bear to think of showing her face at Ashland Middle School on Monday.

About an hour later, the doorbell rang. She heard her mother answer, voices murmuring together, and feet on the staircase. And then there was a knock at her bedroom door and it was Emily and Lindsey, still in their cheerleading uniforms.

If they noticed Alex's face was swollen and blotchy from crying, they pretended not to. "How's your chin?" asked Emily, moving into the room and sprawling onto Alex's bed.

"A little better," said Alex in a tiny voice. She couldn't believe they were speaking to her in such a normal way. "How was the pep rally?"

"It was pretty fun," Lindsey said.

"How did Molly do?"

"She was good," said Emily. "Her ankle seems

to be better and better. I think she's going to be a really nice addition to the team."

"We're all leaving for the game together around six," said Lindsey. "You're going to come, right?"

Alex nodded. "I guess I have to. My dad's the coach and my brother's a player. But I'll sit with my mom. I understand."

"But the whole team is sitting together!" said Emily. "You have to come!"

"I'm not on the team anymore," said Alex. "Remember how I quit?"

Emily and Lindsey exchanged looks.

"Tell her," said Lindsey.

"Tell me what?"

"We had a team meeting after the pep rally," said Lindsey. "No one's mad at you. Not even Rosa. She knows it was an accident. And we understand why you decided to resign, although Em and I are sad about it. But then we proposed that you should be our public relations person. Like, head up the fund-raising for our new uniforms, and do the posters for all the pep rallies. That kind of thing."

"Public relations?" breathed Alex. Her heart leaped with joy. "I'd be perfect for that job!"

"We know," said Emily with a laugh. "That's just what we told Coach Jen, and the rest of the team agreed!"

"The first thing I'll do is make sure everyone's new uniform is properly fitted," said Alex excitedly. "Even a quarter of an inch in the hem, or a simple tuck in the waist, can make a huge difference in the way the uniform fits each person. Plus, the other day I saw some absolutely adorable polka-dot ribbon at the craft store that would totally go with our colors!"

Lindsey and Emily both smiled.

"I can be ready for the game in ten minutes!" said Alex, and galloped off to get dressed.

# CHAPTER FOURTEEN

"Are you sure you're okay?" Ava's friend Kylie asked her again. "You seem extra nervous tonight."

Ava and Kylie were in the stands, waiting for the Tigers' game to begin. Ava was glad to see Alex was at the game too. She knew her sister hadn't gone to school, but obviously she'd talked their mom into letting her go to the game.

Ava had made the decision not to talk to Alex—she didn't want her sister to know that something was bothering her. It was too hard to keep that sort of thing from her twin. Alex would be able to sense how nervous Ava was. What if something went wrong with Tommy's plan? What if Coach somehow found out that he was sneaking out of the stadium to go to his band concert? And she, Ava, was going to help him with the whole thing. She glanced down at the small duffel bag at her feet for the fourth time. It was there. It had Tommy's music and a change of clothes in it. Plus, to add to her general sense of unease, she had the date with Jack to look forward to after the game.

"I'm fine," she said with a weak smile. "Just nervous about the game. Coach thinks it's going to be a close one. And also . . ." She hesitated. Then she decided she might as well share. "And also, I have a kind of, sort of date with Jack after the game, at Sal's."

Kylie gave a low whistle. "Wow! Good for you! Is that why you have lip gloss and an actual shirt on rather than your usual football jersey?"

Ava felt herself flush. "That was Alex's doing," she said. "She laid the whole outfit out for me last night—including the lip gloss. Does it look stupid?"

"No," said Kylie. "You look really nice. I mean it."

"Thanks," said Ava. "I hope this isn't a bad idea. We really like hanging out together. I just don't know if he looks at me as girlfriend material. Or if I look at him that way, to be honest. I don't want to spoil things."

"Stop overthinking it," said Kylie, lightly whacking Ava on the arm. "And stop talking. It's kickoff time, and I want to concentrate on the game."

Ava grinned. Her friend had come so far in such a short time! When they'd first met, Kylie couldn't have explained the difference between a punt and a field goal.

The game was close, and the score toward the end of the first half was 7–7. As the clock ticked down to the halftime, Ava could feel herself tensing up. Twice she saw Tommy glance up at her in the stands from the sidelines. He looked grimly determined. *I guess he's not backing down,* thought Ava.

At halftime, Ava stood up quickly. "Be right back," she said to Kylie. "I'm going to run to the bathroom before the lines get crazy."

Kylie nodded, hardly looking up. She liked to stick around for the halftime show, which was still her favorite part of every game. But then she glanced back at Ava. "What's in the gym bag?" she asked casually.

Ava had slung Tommy's bag over her shoulder. She glanced down at it. "Oh, this? Just some stuff my brother wanted me to drop off."

Kylie shrugged and looked back at the show. That seemed to satisfy her, luckily.

As the band marched out onto the field, Ava wound her way down through the crowded stands and to the locker room area.

About four minutes later, Tommy emerged from the locker room. He'd taken off his pads and uniform and was wearing a T-shirt and sweats. He saw her immediately and took her by the elbow. They moved down the hall and ducked around a corner.

"Here," said Ava, handing him the bag, which he slung onto his own shoulder. "How did it go?"

"Pretty well," he said. "I ran ahead of the team to the locker room. When Coach came in, I told him I'd just puked and that I should probably get out of there. He bought it. I guess he was so distracted by the game, he barely seemed to hear me."

Ava felt like *she* was going to puke.

"So remember the plan," said Tommy. "If he gets home first and asks where I am, you tell him I called Luke and he took me to the walk-in clinic. I texted you to tell you this because I didn't want to bother him or Mom."

Ava nodded, swallowing hard. "Okay. Good luck at the concert."

Tommy glanced at his phone. "Thanks. I better run. Luke's waiting at the side exit. Text me and let me know what happens in the game."

Ava said she would. He gave her a quick Tom version of a hug—enveloping her head in the crook of his elbow—and off he went.

She watched him hustle away down the empty, dimly lit hallway. Outside, she could hear the band still playing, and the shouts of the cheerleaders. She hurried back to her seat.

The Tigers ended up winning, but it was a close game. Ava texted Tommy the final score, and while still holding her phone, she got a message from Jack saying he'd meet her at the gate closest to the Tigers' bench.

"I can't go to Sal's tonight," said Kylie. "It's my sister's birthday, and we're having cake at my house. But I want to hear all about how it went tomorrow, okay?"

Ava nodded. "I promise."

Kylie left, and Alex appeared.

"Exciting game, wasn't it?" said Alex. "It's a shame Tommy didn't get in."

Ava nodded. "Yeah, a shame." She had been wondering whether Alex would notice that Tommy hadn't been on the sidelines for the second half. Apparently she hadn't.

"So, are you ready for your big date?" Alex asked Ava.

Ava rolled her eyes. "No. Have I mentioned how annoying it is that you were the one who created this annoying situation?"

"Yes. Several times. And I said I was sorry . . . kind of." Alex told Ava her news. How she'd confessed to Coach Jen and to the team.

Ava's jaw dropped. "Are we in trouble?"

"You definitely are not. I convinced Coach Jen that you weren't to blame; that I was the evil mastermind. She accepted that. And to be honest, even though we could have gotten away with it, I'm glad she knows. I couldn't have that guilt hanging over my head every second. I swear, Ave, I'm never lying again."

Ava thought about what Tommy was doing at that moment. She shifted uncomfortably.

"And," said Alex, "guess what?" She told Ava about being the PR person for the cheer squad.

"That's so awesome," said Ava warmly. "And how did it go, sitting with the team?"

"Pretty well, except that Annelise kept thanking me for my bravery and courage, and telling everyone how I'd heroically saved her from a terrible injury. Obviously the whole thing was my fault, but she's such a sweet person, she couldn't see that."

Ava's phone buzzed. It was Jack again. "Guess I'd better go," she said.

"Yes. Hurry," said Alex. "I saw him down there waiting for you. I think he actually combed his hair."

Somehow this made Ava feel embarrassed and squeamish. She didn't like how she and Jack were both doing stuff they didn't usually do—she'd never seen his unruly hair neatly combed, and she certainly never wore makeup (unless she was pretending to be her sister, of course). As she made her way down the stadium steps, she realized she hadn't even thought to text Charlie. She usually texted him after the Tigers' games. On the other hand, he hadn't texted her, either.

Jack was waiting for her, and his hair was definitely neater than it usually was.

"Hi," she said, feeling suddenly shy.

"Hi," he said.

They were silent. They watched people moving past them, heading for the exits.

Finally Jack came up with something to say. "So, are you hungry?"

"Um, yeah. A little," said Ava.

"Cool. Let's head to Sal's," said Jack, and Ava nodded in agreement.

What was the matter with her? It was like she'd forgotten how to have a normal conversation. And with Jack, of all people, who was so easy to talk to, usually. Well, he seemed to be having the same problem. On top of feeling awkward about the date, she was nervous about timing. What if this silly thing lasted a long time? What if she didn't get home before Coach? There was almost always someone they knew at Sal's who lived close to the Sacketts and who was willing to give her and Alex a ride on Friday nights. Most everyone understood that the coach's daughters might need a ride home because their dad was busy after the game. But would Jack want to take her home? Was that what happened on a date?

They walked to the pizza parlor without

speaking. Jack was one of those people who seemed comfortable with silence, and normally Ava didn't mind it either, but tonight everything felt weird. She glanced at the time on her phone. She'd be fine. Usually it was at least two hours from the end of the game until Coach got home, sometimes much more than that. He did a post-game talk with the team, and then had inter-views with the media, and then generally met with his assistant coaches to recap the game and watch film and stuff. But with her luck, maybe tonight would be the one night that he chose to go directly home, out of concern for his "sick" kid.

Or—and now she was really torturing herself—what if Coach texted her mom? Maybe told her to cancel her dinner with her friend and go home to check on Tom? It would be equally bad—possibly worse—if their mom were the one to discover the plot. Ava shuddered just thinking about it.

At Sal's, Ava and Jack waved to the table full of their mutual friends but chose a booth in a far corner. They ordered sodas, and Sal himself delivered them, singing an aria in his boom-ing tenor voice. It sounded like a love aria, and Ava didn't like the way Sal looked at the two of them, waggling his thick eyebrows in a silly kind of way.

They sat in silence, sipping their drinks. Ava fiddled with the little accordion-scrunched paper from her straw and racked her brains for something to say. Then finally she thought of something.

"So did you see how PJ had twenty-five completions?"

While at the exact same time, Jack said, "I think Jeff Coolidge rushed for over a hundred yards."

"Sorry, what?"

"Sorry, didn't mean to interrupt."

Ava took another sip of her soda and saw that out of the corner of her eye, several of Jack's friends were making goofy faces at him from their table. Could this be more awkward?

Just when she thought it couldn't possibly, the door chime tinkled and someone walked into the restaurant. Glad to have a distraction, Ava turned to see who it was. Her jaw dropped.

It was Charlie. Her sort-of boyfriend from back in Massachusetts.

# CHAPTER FIFTEEN

Alex was in mid-sip of her drink when Charlie Weidner walked into Sal's. She nearly spewed soda all over the table.

"Are you okay?" asked Emily, slapping Alex on the back several times.

Alex managed to stop coughing enough to gasp that she was fine, that she'd just swallowed a sip the wrong way.

Charlie hadn't seen her yet. He stood near the door, scanning the crowd. A few kids looked up at him curiously. Despite her shock, it struck Alex that it really was obvious when someone showed up who wasn't from Ashland. She couldn't put her finger on why—Charlie wasn't dressed in different clothes or anything. He was still the same freckled, red-haired kid she remembered, although he seemed to have grown at least two inches since she'd last seen him. But somehow he looked like he wasn't from around here.

She glanced over at where Ava was sitting with Jack. Ava had definitely seen Charlie walk in, because she'd picked up the huge menu no one ever looked at—everyone always ordered the specialty, pizza margherita—and had it propped up in front of her. She was clearly hiding behind it. Alex saw her sister's eyes peek out over the top of the menu, and she could tell that Ava was completely freaked out.

"Do you know that kid?" asked Lindsey, looking curiously at Charlie.

"Yes," said Alex. "That's . . . Charlie."

Corey looked up sharply from where he was sitting, farther down the table. Everyone was now staring from Alex to Charlie and back again.

"I thought you said you'd broken up!" hissed Emily under her breath.

"We did," Alex responded weakly.

"So he came all the way from Boston to beg you to come back to him?" asked Emily. "Wow. That is so totally romantic."

Alex stood up. "Be right back," she said to her friends, and she hurried over to where Charlie was standing.

"Charlie? Oh my gosh! I can't believe it!" she gushed, giving him a huge bear hug.

"Hey, Alex," said Charlie. He half hugged her in return, patting her awkwardly on the back.

"What are you doing here?"

"Surprise, ha ha. How's it going? What happened to your chin?"

"Oh, I fell. You know me, I'm a total klutz! But—" Her eyes flicked to Ava's booth. She was still hiding behind the menu. "But what—how—how did you—"

"I'm here with the whole family," said Charlie. "We have a week off at school and we're heading to Mexico. But our connecting flight doesn't leave until midnight tonight, so my mom and your mom are having dinner. And Isabel and I told her not to tell so we could surprise you guys. Izzie's got a temperature, so she's with my dad, but she told me to be sure to say hi to you. She's really upset she doesn't get to see you."

"Wow, that's awesome! Except the part about Izzie being sick, that's not awesome," said Alex, blinking rapidly, trying to think. She needed to look happy to see him, for his sake, but not too happy, because she was aware that an entire table full of her friends was watching how she interacted with this pretend ex-boyfriend, the guy she'd told everyone in the whole school she'd recently broken up with. *And then what do I do about Ava?*

"So where's Ave?" asked Charlie, looking around.

"Ave?"

"Ava."

"Ava?"

"Yeah. Your twin sister?"

"Oh! Ava! Why she's, uh, well, let's see. Where is she?" Alex was madly stalling for time. She prayed that Ava would have the sense to crawl between the tables and get to the bathroom. Then she could shimmy out an open window and escape down the water pipe.

"Charlie!" It was Ava. She'd set down her menu and was calling to him and waving from across the room.

Alex closed her eyes and inhaled a long, cleansing breath. She couldn't believe this was happening.

Charlie gently moved past Alex to head over

to Ava, who was now standing up and walking over to them. Jack stood up too and was looking at Charlie with serious confusion. Ava had a fake frozen smile on her face, as though she were into the third hour of cheerleading tryouts. This time, though, her face was as white as paper.

Alex briefly contemplated running, but then turned and followed after Charlie.

"Hi!" said Ava when she reached Charlie and Alex. She gave Charlie a quick hug, and then they both jumped backward. "What—what are you doing here?"

Charlie explained quickly.

"Oh. So that explains the mysterious date our mom had with an old friend," said Ava. "She was weird about not giving any details."

"Yeah," said Charlie. "We thought it would be cool to surprise you guys."

"Ha-ha, what a surprise," said Ava. It was a hollow laugh. The conversation faltered, and then ground to a standstill. The three stood in awkward silence.

Alex looked from one to the other, wondering what to do. Finally, when the silence between Ava and Charlie became intolerable, she blurted, "So, Charlie. See that guy over there that Ava was sitting with? He's on the school paper. And he's interviewing Ava. About being the only girl on the football team. It's not like a date or anything. Right, Ava?"

Ava's mouth fell open. She looked over her shoulder at Jack. Then she turned back to Charlie.

Jack must have seen the look and interpreted it as an invitation to come join them, which he then did.

"Jack! This is Charlie. Charlie, this is Jack," said Alex desperately.

"Hey, Charlie," said Jack with an easy grin. "I've heard a lot about you."

"You have?" asked Charlie.

"Yep. Alex has talked about you a lot."

"Alex has?"

"Oh, you know my sister," said Ava, jumping in quickly. "Always the chatterbox."

"Um, yeah," said Charlie. "So are you and Jack still talking, or do you have time to hang out?" Charlie asked Ava.

Ava turned bright pink.

Charlie turned to Jack. "I'm impressed you don't need to write anything down. I would never be able to remember what people said."

Jack looked puzzled. "Write it down?"

Ava pulled her phone out and looked down. "Oh, wow, it actually looks like I have to go, you guys," she said. "My brother's texting me and he really needs my help with a, um, a situation, and I'm going to catch a ride back with the Cahills over there, who look like they're heading out. Sorry, Jack. Gotta go. Bye! So awesome to see you, Charlie!"

And she fled.

Alex shot her a reproachful look, but Ava was already on her way out the door. Alex stood there awkwardly between Charlie and Jack, conscious of the fact that Corey and Lindsey and Emily were all looking curiously at the three of them from the long table across the restaurant.

"So, uh, Jack," said Charlie, "Alex says you're an ace reporter for the paper. That's awesome."

Jack looked at Alex and raised an eyebrow.

Alex looked at him and pleaded with her eyes for him to go along with this.

He seemed to understand, because he turned to Charlie and grinned. "Oh, yeah, well, thanks. I try."

Alex felt a surge of gratitude toward Jack.

"Well, Alex, our moms are having dinner

together right down the street at a place called the Pain or something."

"Le pehn," Alex corrected him automatically, pronouncing it the French way. Yes! A way out! "Why don't I walk you there?" she suggested. "We can talk on the way, and catch up and stuff."

Charlie nodded, and after saying good-bye to Jack, Alex led Charlie out. She turned toward the table where her friends were sitting and gave them what she hoped was a look that said, *I'll try to let the poor guy down easy*, before they walked out the door.

# CHAPTER SIXTEEN

As soon as the Cahills had dropped Ava off, she raced inside and discovered with relief that no one was home yet. Moxy started running in circles around Ava the second she stepped into the house.

For twenty minutes Ava sat on the floor, petting Moxy, who, pleasantly surprised to be given such attention, rolled onto her back with all four paws in the air, the better to allow Ava to stroke her tummy. Ava was lost in thought. She still couldn't believe Charlie had shown up at Sal's. Just as she'd finally decided she would break up with him once and for all. Was it a sign of some sort?

Ava was still sitting on the floor with Moxy

when she heard a car door close quietly and Tommy's voice saying thank you to Luke.

Moxy bounded to her feet, and the two of them went to meet him as he came in through the side door.

He tiptoed quietly into the room and looked warily around. "Hey, Ave," he whispered. "Anyone else home yet?" He was dressed in very un-Tommy-like clothes: a dark shirt, a sport coat, and blue jeans.

Ava shook her head. "You better change out of those clothes, though, before they get here," she said.

"Yep, and I should be lying down in my room anyway," he said. "Come up and talk to me in a minute. I'll tell you how it went."

When Ava went upstairs, she found Tommy under the covers of his bed, propped up on his pillows. She went in and sat down.

"So, how was it?"

His dark eyes danced. "It was brilliant, Ave. We won the contest! We totally stole the show! The three of us—Jackson on drums, Harley on bass, and me—each had a solo improv, and we killed it."

"Aw, Tommy, that's so great," said Ava. "But

what are you going to say to Coach?"

"Nothing, I hope," he said. "I'll just say I've been home throwing up but now I feel better."

Alex and Mrs. Sackett were the next to arrive home, followed soon after by Coach. Ava wasn't in the mood to hear about Charlie from Alex, so she pretended to be asleep. She heard her parents go in to check on Tommy, and then she heard the murmur of his voice, sounding weak and sick. She heaved a sigh of relief. It looked like Tommy had gotten away with skipping out on the second half of the game.

"Well, it looks like you got away with it," snapped Alex as she came into Ava's room the next morning without even knocking. She dropped into Ava's comfy chair and crossed her arms, eyeing her sister with extreme annoyance.

Ava was still in bed, but she'd been awake for a while. She closed her phone. "Got away with what?"

"Oh, brother," snorted Alex. "With being on a date with a guy and having the other guy you've been going out with show up at the same exact time? Thanks to me, anyway. I covered for you, even though you were zero help in this whole thing, thank you very much." She sat breathing heavily, her nostrils flaring.

"Al, it's not like I asked for this date with Jack," Ava pointed out. "May I remind you that you were the one who said yes, posing as me?"

"Okay, well, whatever," said Alex. "I am totally and completely exhausted from all the excitement of these past few days."

"I just texted Jack," said Ava quietly. "I apologized for running out like that. Told him maybe we should stick to playing basketball together. He was pretty decent about it."

"Wait. So you broke it off with Jack?"

"Well, it's not like there was anything to break off," Ava pointed out. "We weren't actually dating. But now I'm conflicted about Charlie again. I don't know what to think about the fact that he came all that way, just to see me."

Alex shifted uncomfortably. "Hey, Ave. Have you been on his Buddybook page recently?"

"No. You know I don't go on Buddybook nearly as often as you do."

"I know. That's why I'm mentioning this," said Alex. "See, it looks to me like Charlie might kind of have a girlfriend. Remember Caroline Blatz from last year?"

"Caroline the volleyball star?"

Alex nodded.

Ava sat, contemplating. "She's okay, I guess. Still, it's weird. You finally decide you're going to break up with someone, and then find out they were about to break up with you, and it feels, well, bad. But I'm glad for him."

Alex watched Ava open her phone and send a text. Soon after, her phone buzzed, and then she sent another.

"Who's it from?" Alex asked.

"Charlie. I just texted him and apologized for being weird at Sal's and said how good it was to see him. And then he texted me and said one of the reasons he wanted to sit and talk with me last night was that he wanted me to know he'd sort of started going out with Caroline. And I texted back and said I knew, and it's cool. So we're cool."

"So you just went from having two boyfriends to zero boyfriends—and you're happy about it?" Alex asked, shaking her head. "I just don't understand how we can be sisters, let alone identical twins."

Ava grinned. "It's a wonder."

# CHAPTER SEVENTEEN

The next day Ava joined her parents and Alex on the sidelines after her game. Flushed and sweaty, she was exhilarated by the win over the Titans.

"Nice game, Fourteen," said Coach, whacking her affectionately on her padded shoulder.

She grinned happily. "It was a tough one, but I thought we played pretty well."

"And you caught a thirteen-yard pass!" exclaimed Mrs. Sackett.

"Wait. Was she a wide receiver today?" asked Alex. "I somehow missed that."

Ava and Coach exchanged a bemused look.

"Yes, honey, she played wide receiver for

almost a full quarter and did really well," said Mrs. Sackett.

"Well, congrats!" said Alex.

"Here comes Mr. Kelly," said Mrs. Sackett under her breath.

Ava didn't like the look in Mr. Kelly's eyes. She knew he didn't approve of her dad's coaching tactics, and now that she was playing wide receiver, she knew he also resented her taking playing time away from his nephew. He always acted nice around her dad, but Ava didn't buy it.

"Great game, young lady!" said Mr. Kelly as he joined the Sacketts. He raised his hat briefly as he nodded to Mrs. Sackett. "Y'all just cleaned their plow today!"

"Um, thanks?" Ava ventured, not sure if he'd meant it as a compliment.

"Howdy, Coach."

"Doug," Coach said with a nod.

"Say, how's that son of yours? I noticed he wasn't on the sidelines for the second half of the game last night."

"Oh, he's just fine," said Coach. "Tom got sick during the game. It was a sudden onset kind of thing. I sent him home to bed, but luckily, it seems like it was just a twelve-hour bug."

Mr. Kelly pushed his half-glasses down his nose and fixed Coach with a beady stare. An uneasy sensation shot up and down Ava's spine; she had a feeling Mr. Kelly was enjoying himself.

"You don't say," he said. "Well, I heard from Gladys Pike that there was a big band competition over at Eastern High last night. And she says your son was in that competition. And that he plum won it. Now isn't that the darnedest thing? Wonder how on earth she'd think she'd seen that son of yours, when you're standing right here, tellin' me he took ill."

With a triumphant smile, Mr. Kelly crossed his arms across his burly chest and looked at Coach innocently.

Ava felt her heart plummet into her cleats. She heard Alex, next to her, give a little gasp of surprise. Her mother looked at Coach.

Coach's expression did not change, though. He merely nodded at Mr. Kelly and said, "Well, that Gladys Pike surely is a staunch supporter of the arts. Glad she enjoyed the concert. And now we Sacketts need to get this one home. Good to see you, Doug."

And Ava felt his guiding hand on her back, propelling her toward the parking lot. Alex and

Mrs. Sackett followed them.

They rode home in silence.

When they got to their house, Coach walked in ahead of them and took the stairs three at a time. Ava heard the door to Tommy's room open and close, and the murmuring of voices.

"Do you girls know anything about this?" asked Mrs. Sackett.

"Mom! No! Of course not!" said Alex quickly. "Mr. Kelly was just making trouble. Tommy went home from the game. He was sick. Right, Ave?"

Ava didn't say anything. She just stared down at her feet.

Mrs. Sackett gave Ava a long look. "Go upstairs, Ava," she said quietly. "We'll discuss this later."

Ava ran upstairs and quickly showered. As she turned off the water, she heard Tommy and Coach's voices much louder. They were arguing. She couldn't make out the words, but of course, she didn't need to. She quickly threw on clothes and went to see Alex.

Alex was sitting on her bed, her eyes wide,

clutching her pillow closely. "Ave! Did you know about it?" she asked in a whisper.

Ava nodded. "Yeah. It was really important to him, Al. But wow, I feel terrible. Lying can really get you into big trouble. It's not worth it."

Alex nodded. "Even if you don't get caught. That's why I confessed to Coach Jen about trading places. I couldn't take the guilt. Tommy did get caught, and it sounds way worse than if he'd just gone and told Coach the truth."

They heard Tommy's door open, and the shouting grew louder. Then they heard feet stomping down the stairs, and the front door slammed.

"I think that was Tommy!" whispered Alex.

Ava just nodded. "This is bad, Al," she said.

# CHAPTER EIGHTEEN

Ava lay awake past midnight that night, thinking about everything that had happened. Tommy hadn't returned. She could hear her parents in their room talking. She lay awake, listening to the night sounds outside. Then at last, at about 12:20 in the morning, she heard the kitchen door open and knew Tommy was finally home. There was a *cathunk* of the refrigerator door being opened. *Cathunk* as it closed. Dishes, silverware clanking. In her parents' room, the talking had stopped. Were they asleep? Or listening to the sounds of Tommy making himself a midnight snack?

She thought about going to see her brother

but then changed her mind. She heard his foot-steps coming up the stairs. The door of his room closed. Then the house was quiet.

Sunday morning Ava woke up early, but Tommy's room was empty, his bed a rumpled heap of sheets. She headed down to the kitchen, but it was empty too. Her mother had left a note on the kitchen table saying she was out for a long run. Through the window over the sink, Ava could see Coach outside in the backyard, hammering something on the battered old door of the shed.

She texted Tommy.

Where are you?

He did not reply for a full five minutes. Then:

I'm practicing. At the church.

Ava ate a quick bowl of cereal and went outside to see Coach.

"Morning," he said shortly, without pausing in his hammering. He had added a crosspiece of wood to the back of the door of the shed and was hammering it into place. In his baggy, faded jeans and black, faded-to-gray T-shirt, Ava thought her dad looked like a teenager. He could be Tommy's twin, at least from the back.

She sat on an overturned bucket and watched her dad finish his task. When at last he began picking up his tools, she said, "Hey, Coach? Want to go for a walk with me?"

He cocked an eyebrow at her. "Sure, honey. Where to?"

"Just . . . not far. I want to show you something."

He held her gaze for a moment, as though sizing up her earnestness, and said, "Let me put these tools away. I'll meet you in front in five."

They set off in silence, Ava leading the way down the block. It was early enough that they didn't meet any neighbors, and only one vehicle passed them, a beat-up old pickup truck stacked high with fat sacks of grain. Ava didn't know what Tommy had told Coach about his concert and his scheme. Did Coach know she had been Tommy's accomplice? Was he angry with her, too? Knowing Tommy, he would have told Coach only whatever was absolutely necessary, but knowing Coach, he had gotten to the truth by asking just the right perceptive questions. She kept quiet.

A few blocks later Ava saw the church, a pretty little building with weather-beaten white siding and a simple steeple. The sign out front said that the next service was at noon, and it was just past nine.

As they drew closer, Ava could hear some very unchurchlike music: jazzy, syncopated rhythms and an upbeat melody. Next to her, Coach stopped and stood still. Ava looked up at him. He had the strangest mixture of emotions playing across his face—like the toy kaleidoscope she had owned and loved as a little kid. You twisted it and wild colors and patterns morphed and emerged and changed into other patterns. Passing across her father's face, one after another, Ava could see anger change to pride, then exasperation, then admiration, then weary resignation as he stood listening to Tommy play.

"Coach?" she asked softly, squeezing his hand a little. "Do you want to go inside?"

He looked down at her, startled, as though he'd forgotten she was there. "Yes," he said, and the two of them climbed the front stairs and entered the church through the heavy wooden double doors.

From the back of the empty church, they stood still again and listened to Tommy play. He was so engrossed in his piece he didn't seem to have heard them come in. But as they made their way down the side aisle toward the piano—a gleaming black baby grand—Tommy looked up, and the music stopped. He sat quietly, watching them approach, his face impassive.

Ava tugged on Coach's shirt. "Should I leave you guys alone?" she whispered.

He looked down at her, nodded, and ruffled her hair.

She turned and headed back outside to sit on the front steps of the church. It faced east, and the warm, late morning sun glinted off the stained-glass windows.

After a few minutes, Coach emerged and stood next to her on the top of the stoop. They didn't speak, but Ava could feel that he wasn't too mad. Maybe not mad at all.

"Do you want to head home?" Coach asked her.

"Maybe in a little while," said Ava.

Coach nodded. Ava knew he understood she wanted to stay behind to talk with Tommy. She watched her dad trot down the steps and turn toward their house, his long, lanky stride showing how much of an athlete he still was.

A few moments later the door opened behind her, and Tommy sat down next to her on the step. They sat in silence. Then she said, "How did it go?"

"As well as could be expected," said Tommy. "I'm suspended for two games, but he had to do that, and I knew it—he can't treat me differently from any of the other players. I told him I love football, but I also love music, and he accepted that."

"That's great," said Ava.

"Yeah, I think he's even a little proud of me. He's not proud of the fact that I lied and that Mr. Kelly knows it. But he knows I won't pull that again. After the season's over, I'll have a lot more time, obviously, to rehearse."

"That's awesome, Tommy," said Ava. "You want to walk to the park and shoot around with me?"

"Nah, I've got a while before they start showing up for the next service here, so I'm going to keep practicing. But I'll catch you later."

Ava went to the park anyway, and saw Jack shooting around. She approached cautiously, because she wasn't sure how things stood between them. When he saw her, he bounce-passed her the ball, and she drove in for a reverse layup.

"Lucky," he said with a grin. "Get warmed up and I'll whup you in one-on-one."

Ava smiled back and started dribbling.

Jack won the first game, and Ava the second. They were just about to start the tiebreaker when Ava spotted Alex approaching, walking Moxy. When Moxy saw Ava, she tugged at the leash, and Alex dropped it, allowing Moxy to bound across the play area toward Ava.

Jack held the ball while Ava petted Moxy. He shook his head as Alex approached. "I forget how much you two look alike," he said. "Sometimes it's really hard to tell you guys apart."

"Good thing we don't dress alike," said Ava, shooting Alex a mischievous glance.

Alex smiled back. "Yeah, good thing."

# Ready for more
# ALEX AND AVA?

Here's a sneak peek at the next
book in the It Takes Two series:

# Even the
# Score

*This is no big deal*, Ava Sackett thought. Then she turned and sprinted away from the boys.

Her heart beat in rhythm with her feet. Thin lines of sweat trickled down her neck from the heat of the September Texas sun. Her fingertips tingled with anticipation. She sensed the coaches on the sidelines watching. *Today is my big chance,* she thought. *A chance to show I can do more than kick a football.*

She was now the official kicker of the Ashland Tiger Cubs. She was also the first girl in the history of Ashland Middle School to make the football team.

Not that any other girl had tried out.

She knew some boys in the halls had been whispering about her. They said that her being on the team was a pity thing or a special consideration, because her dad coached the high school team. Her twin sister Alex told her not to listen to them.

"You're good at football. Really good. Better-than-most-boys good," Alex insisted. And when Ava kicked the thirty-three-yard field goal at the game last Saturday, those boys finally stopped whispering.

"I'm going to try mixing things up," Coach Kenerson announced at practice today. "Ava, you go in for Ethan at wide receiver."

She couldn't hold back her grin. Finally! A chance to be a part of the action.

Wide receivers needed to be superfast to catch the pass from the quarterback and then sprint down the field for a touchdown. Running wasn't a problem for Ava. She'd always been fast. Her mom said she ran before she learned to walk. Ava flexed her fingers, readying herself for the catch.

Corey O'Sullivan, the quarterback, torpedoed the ball toward the other wide receiver, Owen Rooney. Ava wished Corey had sent it her way, but he'd made the right choice. She was surrounded, while no defenders blocked Owen. It was an easy grab-and-go.

Ava watched the ball land in Owen's outstretched hands. Then he pivoted his shoulders suddenly, and just as suddenly, the ball dropped onto the grass. Defenders dove in for the interception.

"Are you kidding me?" Coach K bellowed. He threw up his stocky arms in disbelief. Owen, their star wide receiver, had bungled the easy play.

Again.

Coach K marched across the field until he stood an inch away from Owen. He pressed his face close to Owen's helmet. "What is with you this week? These are Pee Wee catches. Baby stuff. Where's your focus?"

Owen shrugged and stared at his cleats.

Even across the field, Ava saw Owen's face flame. His wiry body tensed as the coach yelled. Ava felt bad for him. Owen was usually able to catch the trickiest passes, but his technique had been sloppy all week.

As Coach K returned to the sidelines, Owen glanced toward her. She met his gaze, hoping to send a silent encouragement. She and Alex always did this across a crowded room, and it worked.

Must be an identical twin thing, Ava decided, because Owen scowled at her, then turned away.

Ava jogged back to the line of scrimmage. Was he angry that Coach K had also put her in at his position? She'd moved to Ashland, Texas, from Massachusetts this summer and didn't know Owen well enough to know how competitive he was.

They ran the drill again. Ava sprinted into the backfield, hoping to find an open pocket. She heard defenders alongside her. Her focus stayed on Corey as he set up for the pass. Once again, he targeted Owen.

Ava's gaze moved to Owen. For a split second, she thought he glanced back at her. She shook her head. That couldn't be right. A wide receiver would never take his eyes off the ball.

Then Owen stumbled. He caught himself quickly, but not before the football landed five feet behind him.

Coach K paced the sidelines, muttering loudly. Corey jogged over to Owen. "What's the deal, O? Those are perfect passes I'm sending you."

Owen shrugged, then snuck another quick glance toward Ava.

Corey kicked at the grass. This was the closest Ava had ever seen him come to losing his cool. "Come on, O! Work with me."

"Rooney!" Coach K called. "Move yourself to tight end."

"But Coach, I always play wide receiver on the left," Owen protested.

"This time you're not." Coach Kenerson blew his whistle. "Get in alongside Sackett."

Owen hurried next to Ava. She tried to catch his eye, maybe give him a thumbs-up or something, but now he wouldn't even look her way. The whistle sounded, and the center snapped the ball. Ava took off. Owen raced alongside her, keeping pace.

They matched each other in speed. Ava tracked the arc of the football while her feet stayed in motion. The ball headed toward her. Her heart pounded with anticipation as she readied to make the catch.

If she nailed this, maybe Coach K would put her in more games. Up until now, he'd been nervous about having her on the field where she could get tackled. That girl thing again! But she wasn't afraid. Her dad and her older brother, Tommy, had taught her how take a hit. Plus, she was fast. These boys had no chance of catching her once that ball was cradled in her arms.

*Come on, come on,* she chanted silently as the ball soared toward her. She sensed Owen only inches away, hovering by her side. Why was he so close? Didn't he trust her to make the catch?

She squinted into the sun and reached up. As her fingertips brushed the ball's worn leather, something hooked her ankle. Her feet flew up, and she landed with a surprising thud on the ground. Her stomach twisted as the ball rolled out of reach.

An incomplete pass.

She whipped her head around. Owen was sprawled next to her, his cleat suspiciously close to her ankle.

"Did you trip me?" Ava asked.

"S-sorry," Owen stammered. He pulled away from her. "I got too close."

Before she could reply, Coach K towered over them. His mirrored sunglasses hid his eyes. "Rooney! Sackett! Are you two confused?"

"Confused?" Ava repeated.

"Did you think this was a clown routine at the circus?" He ran his fingers through his graying hair. "Do you need me to draw a picture to show you where the wide receiver and tight end are supposed to run?"

"I know where to go," Owen insisted, standing.

"Me too," Ava scrambled to her feet as Coach Kenerson lectured about playing position.

She waited for Owen to tell the coach that it was his mistake, that he'd accidentally tripped her. Owen stayed silent, and Ava fumed. Or maybe it wasn't an accident. Had Owen messed her up on purpose?

"Let's run it again," Ava suggested. She was eager to prove herself.

This time Corey sent the ball right to her. She caught it easily, dodging the defenders nearby.

"That's how it's done!" Coach K cried. "Everyone give me two cooldown laps around the field."

The team set off jogging. Ava and Owen pulled off their helmets and joined the pack.

"Hey, Owen! Want a candy bar?" Xander Browning called loudly.

"Huh?" Owen asked.

"I've got plenty of Butterfingers. Oh, wait, you don't need any of those today, do you?" Xander teased. A couple of guys laughed.

"That's not funny," Ava called back. All players had off days. And off weeks.

"Peanut butter with chocolate is my favorite kind of candy. How about you?" she asked Owen, even though she knew the crack was about his failure to catch and not about a candy bar. She thought he'd appreciate her changing the subject.

He opened his mouth as if to say something. Then he scowled and sprinted forward. He finished half a lap ahead of the rest of the team.

*Owen really doesn't like me,* Ava realized. She wondered why. She usually got along with guys who played sports. Her sister said she "spoke their language." But Owen wasn't speaking to her at all.

Ava gulped from her water bottle and wiped her forehead with a towel. Her short chocolate-brown curls lay matted in sweat. Helmet-head was way worse than regular hat-head! As she tried to fluff them with her fingers, she overheard Ryan O'Hara, the tackle, and Andy Baker, the middle linebacker, behind her.

"Owen looks horrible out there," Ryan complained.

"It's all her fault," Andy whispered.

Ava stiffened. She didn't have to guess who they were talking about. She was the only girl on the field.

"My dad and brother said this is what happens when you let girls play. My brother said they're bad luck on the field," Andy reported.

"You're right!" Ryan sounded as if he'd just discovered a big secret. "She's messing him up."

Ava swallowed hard. She wasn't doing anything to mess up Owen. He was messing up all on his own.

Getting on the team hadn't been easy. She had had to appeal to the school board to give her a fair chance. Now that she'd made it, she just wanted to be like everyone else on the team. She didn't want to be the girl football player.

*This is Texas,* she reminded herself. *People here don't like it when outsiders mess with their football traditions. Girls aren't part of the football tradition.*

Coach K had them gather around and take a knee. She gazed at her teammates. Corey gave her a grin. Most of the guys, like Corey and Xander and their friend Logan Medina, supported her. Big, burly Andy never said anything nice about anyone, so she wasn't surprised that he had a problem with her. She glanced at Owen, always so cool and mellow. She never thought he'd be angry to have her on the team.

". . . we have one job every Saturday," the coach was saying when she tuned back in. "What is it?"

"To win!" they all cried.

"Wrong!" bellowed Coach K. "Our job is to play our best as a team. A team is a group effort. So if you had a bad day, got a bad grade, ate a bad sandwich, that's your deal and you need to leave it behind in the locker room. When you walk onto this field, you walk on as a group. We have a job to do together, so you have to all stop thinking about yourselves and put the good of the team first. Am I clear?"

"Yes, Coach!" they all shouted.

"Great. Tomorrow I expect you to come to practice with better focus and ready to play as a family. Together we will light up that new scoreboard we're getting!"

The team all placed their hands in the middle and yelled, "Go, Cubs!"

Ava chewed her lip as she made her way off the field. Coach K was right. Her dad was always telling his players the same thing. She was too caught up with proving herself. She had to stop worrying and do what was best for the team.

From now on, she'd be a total team player.

**Belle Payton** isn't a twin herself, but she does have twin brothers! She spent much of her childhood in the bleachers reading—er, cheering them on—at their football games. Though she left the South long ago to become a children's book editor in New York City, Belle still drinks approximately a gallon of sweet tea a week and loves treating her friends to her famous homemade mac-and-cheese. Belle is the author of many books for children and tweens, and is currently having a blast writing two sides to each It Takes Two story.

# sew zoey

If you think Alex and Ava are fun, wait until you meet Zoey Webber, a seventh grader turned fashion blogger! Check out the Sew Zoey books, available at your favorite store!